KALLISTA

KALLISTA
The Forbidden One

just Deirdre.

COPYRIGHT

Kallista: The Forbidden One

Written by *just* Deirdre.

Cover Design by Flora (florfi) Figueroa.

Edited by Michelle Rascon, Kit Duncan, and Dara Dumilola.

This is a work of fiction. Names, characters, places, and incidents are either the product of the author's imagination or are used fictitiously, and any resemblance to any actual persons, living or dead, events or locales is entirely coincidental.

Text copyright © 2019 by just Deirdre.
All rights reserved.

No part of this book may be reproduced, or stored in a retrieval system, or transmitted in any form or by any means, electronic, mechanical, photocopying, recording, or otherwise, without express written permission of the publisher.

This is a work of fiction. Names, characters, places, and incidents are either the product of the author's imagination or are used fictitiously, and any resemblance to any actual persons, living or dead, events or locales is entirely coincidental.

Mature audiences only should read this book as its content contains graphic sex and language. Please do not continue reading if you are under the age of 18 or if this content is disturbing to you.

First Edition, Published 2020 by Deirdre Braud

ISBN-13:978-1-7339521-8-7 Ebook
ISBN-13:978-1-7339521-2-5 Paperback
ISBN-13:978-1-7339521-3-2 Hardcover
Library of Congress Control Number: 2019904116

Formatted by: kimolisa(fiverr)

For my children, Glynedra, Glynis,
Delloid (Ajamu) Sr. My daughter-in-law, Sharon.
My brother, Demetrius. My significant other, Earl. My
mother.

TABLE OF CONTENTS

KALLISTA
The Forbidden One

just Deirdre.

1 | KALLISTA

2018 DENVER COLORADO. KALLISTA TURNED and walked out of the house with Blake following closely behind. She wouldn't take her prize under the watchful eyes of all the girls at the party. She swayed her hips seductively sensing the thumping sound of his heart. He desired her, and there was a triumphant feeling to that. His arousal and heightened hormones climaxed her sexuality. It would be a sweet conquest.

A grove of trees just outside the house and toward the backyard was the ideal place for a kill, but first she would have a great deal of fun with his body. Kallista laughed at his excited thoughts. He thought about how he'd never had sex with an older woman and the envy on his buddies' faces when he relayed the experience to them.

He was too engrossed by the swaying motion of her hips and the mounds of her breasts to care about where they were headed. He had just one thing on his mind: burying himself in her gorgeous body. Kallista thought he had quite an imagination, picturing all the different sexual positions he hoped to try out.

"We're here," she said, rousing him from his thoughts.

It was a small clearing, twenty feet of open ground surrounded by a circle of trees, illuminated by the moon. He smiled and she read his mind—he planned to put that beautiful woman's back to a tree and give her the best sex of her life.

In a forceful jerk, he pulled her in close. She liked it rough, so she welcomed his aggressiveness. Kallista gave him an amused look when he pushed her against the closest tree.

"So, what would you like me to do to you?" he asked.

"Lots of nasty things," Kallista said, chuckling.

"Oh, naughty girl, huh? I like it." He paused. "Wait, why are your eyes like that?" He took half a step back.

"Um, they change color when I get excited… I mean, really excited. You must be doing something right," she said, pulling him back closer.

With Kallista's back against the tree, he began to kiss her neck and fondle her breasts with total abandon. He moved his mouth to her chest and his hand to her crotch. The delicious richness of her soft moans washed over him. She buried his other hand in her hair, and he responded by pulling her even closer.

"Enough foreplay. Let's fuck," Blake said.

A look of delight played out on her face. She fixed her now blood-orange eyes on Blake and worked her compulsion. While hearing him scream would be exciting, she would have to pass this time given the circumstances. She needed him willing and pliant, even in the throes of pain.

Before he could blink, she switched positions and pushed him against the tree.

Nervous and unsettled, his eyes opened wide as he stared at her.

Kallista sneered at him and took his lower lip between her mouth. As she held him close, she felt a sizeable erection against her thigh. She found it intriguing and decided it was pointless letting that entire "gift" go to waste. She went on her knees and freed his cock from the constriction of his jeans.

"Oh, yeah! Get that dick!" he said in an exaggerated whisper.

She swaddled her mouth around his cock and sighed blissfully as the first bit of pre-cum cocktail hit her tongue. It was the first time she had her mouth around a man's penis, and she felt utterly exhilarated. All she'd ever known were the gratification that comes with quenching the thirst for blood.

She had heard thoughts and the talk of oral sex, in nightclubs and bars, but she'd never experienced it. Kallista believed nothing could feel more powerful and exciting than draining someone of their blood and their mortality.

But, strangely enough, she seemed to know exactly where to lick and suck to get what she wanted. Sucking dick was as invigorating as drinking blood, which she did her entire life. Until now.

Kallista watched as his eyes rolled to the back of his head. The rapture was intense. Perhaps knowing nothing about her other than her first name made it exciting, the novelty and spontaneity of it all. Nonetheless, she had him bound in a cloud of ecstasy, the likes of which he'd never felt before.

"Oh, God! Oh my God! You're amazing!" he garbled, his body tensing.

Kallista, also captivated by the arousing experience, heard his voice, but it sounded like she was miles away from him. A slight breeze blew her hair as she continued licking and sucking every inch of his shaft. Her body was alive, her breathing was erratic. It was different. She reached a high unlike any she'd ever felt, and when he came, semen flowed down her throat and her cells regenerated. The pinnacle of any ordeal she ever received.

"Whoa! Wait a minute! You're glowing!" he said, after the post-coital euphoria subsided.

"I feel amazing," Kallista responded, taking a pause and returning to her feet. She reveled in the glow that radiated from her body—stroking the smoothness of her skin, flipping her hands over, relishing her newfound youthfulness. Her skin, which worried her moments ago, radiated as if she were a newborn.

She threw her head back and let out a low but wicked laugh. Elated, her thirst more commanding than ever,

Kallista moved like the wind, her speed like lightning. One moment she was right in front of him, and the next second, she was on him like a wild animal. He couldn't have seen her coming. There was no time to protest; the fear was instantaneous, and fright fluttered in his chest.

Terror surged within him, her beautiful Nordic white hair he admired moments ago looked like fire—a bonfire. She pinned him down, her fangs buried deep in his neck. Kallista drank voraciously. The blood was thick and delicious, exactly what she needed after the blissfulness from his cum. She felt a marriage of climactic feelings; it was amazing, animalistic, and primal, and she loved every bit of it. Blake whimpered in pain, and she giggled. His pain brought her pleasure. She drank to fill and did not stop until he took his last breath.

Getting back on her feet, a small trail of blood ran down her lips toward her chin, she licked it off with relish. Her skin still glowed under the bright moonlight. Her fear of aging was gone. She'd discovered her real fountain of youth.

"I will live forever," she said, her voice resonating through the night. Music still blared from the fraternity house, but her surroundings were serene. She looked down at the young man's body. "I will never forget you. One never forgets the first practice." She smiled victoriously as she tiptoed over the body and walked away.

One Hour Earlier

The murky expanse became darker as the humid summer night went on. The sunrays had long since disappeared over the horizon, replaced by thousands of stars. A light breeze rustled the leaves as Kallista looked through the tree branches. Now, the night was dark, and the moon was nowhere to be found.

Kallista heard a party in the distance. She glanced down at her glittering dress. It ended mid-thigh—a perfect outfit for an uninvited party guest. With a raised eyebrow and a deep-seated chuckle, she thought about how women dresses had evolved from the time she was a girl. That said, Kallista never cared for anyone's opinion, nor did she follow the rules of attire—that was all too boring, and she didn't abide by such nonsense.

Walking into the Boulder Colorado Frat house, she took in the whole scene. She owned the room. Bodies rocked to the music, and the alcohol flowed freely. It was exactly as she expected: young men and women in various stages of fornication, bodies intertwined on the dance floor and in dark corners. Kallista could smell the hormones all over the place. She closed her eyes, took a deep breath, and the sexual scent assailed her system, arousing her senses. Kallista's body throbbed with sensation from within. It would be an exciting night.

After a few seconds, all eyes at the party were fixated on her. She had no care in the world to give. She could see the guys checking her out and the young women glancing furtively as they whispered.

"Who is she!? What is she doing here?

"Does anyone know her? Who invited her?"

"Look at her skin, flawless as smooth cream. She is gorgeous."

She was an exquisite woman, with tantalizing silver eyes and a curvaceous body that men would go to war for. Kallista never had to wonder what anyone was thinking. Besides her incredible beauty, she had the ability of telepathy and could plant ideas and thoughts in the minds of others.

No corner of the house was safe from the music's roar. They ran amok, those human children, frolicking anywhere they could. Free rein and it was plain they loved the way it felt. Freedom, Kallista recognized, could be as addictive as a drug, a stage she had already gone past. She went through it a long time ago, not long after she left the coven.

She touched the tip of her tongue to her fangs, and her mouth watered. All she wanted was to eat. It had been a long time since she had blood—nineteen hours, to be exact—and it was time to sate her hunger. A fleeting sense of pity ran through her mind for her next victim, whoever it would be. He or she wouldn't survive the night.

Perplexed, she took a quick glimpse in the massive mirror in the foyer, taking in her albino skin and the faint wrinkles around the eyes. Something about her was changing. For a ninety-five-year-old human, it was expected, but she was a hybrid vampire with the youthfulness of a thirty-year-old; she should not be aging. It was not what she wanted. However, she knew how it worked. She was half-human, and that tainted part of her blood caused her cells to gradually degenerate. Her mother remained the same since her vampire birthing, which was three hundred years ago—or so she liked to brag.

Kallista chased the thought from her mind and focused on the task ahead. Her throat parched with a dry burning sensation, to the extent she already imagined the flow of thick human blood streaming down it and the relief it would bring. It was bound to be glorious; there was nothing more satisfying than feeding after hours of going without feeding.

The party rocked—bottles of alcohol were all over the place, and even more cigarettes. Kallista hated nicotine; its pungent smell reduced the sweetness of human blood. It was easy to spot a smoker from the stale scent coming from beneath their skin, and she was not interested in any of them.

Kallista smiled to herself as she watched the young college students do all the silly things children do— dissolving in laughter, touching their bodies, lacing their fingers, and screaming for no reason.

Then a blue-eyed, ash-blond young man took her out of her fixation with his unabashed and lustful stare. She had a thing for attractive faces, so she went along with it.

Something was exciting about toying with food before eating it.

She pulled her thoughts away from every other person in the room and focused on the young man who stared rather bawdy at her. He stood with his back against the wall, one hand in a pocket and the other holding a bottle of beer. His jeans were deliberately worn but clean, and they fit him well, adding to his lustful demeanor. Her lips parted as her eyes traveled along the lines of his lean body. He was ideal for her. She could see his muscles rippling under the tight outline of his T-shirt, and she instantly knew how the encounter would end. She could feel his body temperature rise from across the room.

Kallista could tell the young man considered himself an alpha male, one of the most popular guys on campus all the girls wanted. Those used to getting all the attention and would discard those who did not meet his standard.

Still observing him, she watched him slowly exhale as his eyes moved from her lips to her breasts, then to her hips, and back up to her lips. She wanted him to desire her with a ferocity that scared him. She wanted him to feel her soft lips against his—it would be the most ridiculous and exciting thing she had ever encountered.

She bit her lower lip subtly, but the way his body responded was not subtle. In no time, he stood upright and headed toward her.

"You are so damn beautiful… but I'm sure you knew that," he said. Kallista liked his smoothness and amused him with a side smile. "It must be my lucky night. I'm Blake," he added.

"It is your night," she said playfully. "*Come with me,*" she said using compulsion—without sound, just voices in his head. That was all it took for him to salivate after her, anticipating the moment.

"I'd follow you anywhere," he said with a dazed expression.

"Yes, you will."

2 | KALLISTA

THE WEATHER WAS PERFECT FOR a walk. It was one of those warm summer afternoons where the world is sunny, and everything looks bright and beautiful. It had been a week since Kallista discovered the secret to her eternal youth. Ever since that moment, a new fervent longing had bloomed inside her, a thirst different and stronger than that of blood. It sprouted from the depths of her soul and blossomed into something she couldn't comprehend. The craving was like that of a junkie needing a fix—hooked and wanted more.

Prowling the city, she searched for a new victim. She wore a skimpy black skirt and a dark blouse with pearl beading along the plunging neckline.

"Hey, beautiful," a deep male voice called behind her. She ignored it and quickened her steps as she walked off the main road into a dark alley.

Empty bottles littered the ground. In the corners, rats scurried all over the place. Garbage bins overflowed with smelly trash, and pallets and boxes lined the brick walls.

"Hey! I'm talking to you," the voice said. "Oh, come on, don't be rude!"

She couldn't picture what he looked like, but the arrogant tone of his voice told her precisely what he was: someone who would not take no for an answer—the type that believed the world owed him something and always had to pay him back.

She walked into the alley and heard him step up behind her.

"I said HEY, you little bitch!"

Kallista stopped and looked back, seeing him now. His crooked nose looked like it had received too many punches. His eyes were beady, resembling one rat she saw scurrying about the alley. He wasn't the best-looking man, but she could feel the craving getting the better of her.

"Hello. Don't be so angry." She pivoted to face him head-on. "I wanted you to follow me. You're handsome, and I'm horny," she said as she ran her hand up her inner thigh, touching herself.

She observed the anger on the man's face change to incredulity and lust within a nanosecond. "I was right. You are a slut," he uttered. "Dressed like that, I knew you had to be one. Come get some of this," he said, cupping his manhood.

Kallista strolled up to him, a lewd smile taking shape on her face. There was an odd smell in the air, but she paid it no mind. An alley strewn with rodents and trash, what more could one expect.

"You don't mind if I put my mouth on it, do you?" She licked her lips.

"Hell, no! I insist!" He gestured with both hands between his legs. "Come here, you dirty little whore, and open your mouth. Don't be shy!"

Offended and agitated anger brimmed inside her, this man would die in the most painful way possible. She smiled maliciously, went on her knees, and took him in her mouth.

"Yeah, take it all in." His head tilted back, and his eyes closed halfway as he said in approval, "Go deeper, get it all in, yeah."

She took her time to tease him in ways unaware were capable of. He gripped her head to fuck her mouth.

"Oh! Yeah! Suck it, cunt! Yeah, right there, Mm-mmm!" he quietly moaned as he came.

The climax ended, but Kallista kept sucking and sucking and sucking.

"Okay, bitch, that's enough!" he said. "Stop!"

Ignoring his plea. Focused on her goal. She was a giant leech stuck on him. He tried pulling her head away, but she resisted with a sinister grin. That's when she noticed her skin glow.

"That's enough! Stop!" he screamed.

She did not stop. Instead, she attacked with new fervor, tightened her lips and sucked harder. He staggered as he became weaker and grabbed a nearby garbage bin. Kallista felt his essence depleting and knew he was only seconds from his demise.

A few seconds later, she stopped, stood, and pushed his body away. Before he let go of the garbage bin and collapsed, she heard his last breath escape. Lying on the ground in a heap, his face was the perfect picture of abject horror.

Satisfied it was better than the first time, she now understood how the process worked.

"To the death," she declared.

3 | JAQLYN

1922. THE FAIR-SKINNED ENGLISH WOMAN stood with her arms akimbo in front of the lab located across the moat from the main chambers. She was the epitome of a melanin goddess—skin that glistened under the rays of the sun to go with her thick black straight hair, piled atop her head in a messy bun. Many things went through her mind, but none reflected on her face.

She looked over at the vampires working in the center of the coven. A lot was wrong in her estimation. They could have been at the top of the food chain, the most powerful creatures on earth. That was how it was meant to be, how it once was. Instead, they seemed satisfied with being a weak, dying breed. Humans had discovered them, and now the end seemed nearer than ever. Immortals hunted like prey. It was shameful.

Overhead, the sun glowed through the stained-glass dome, but the vampires continued to work. Her eyes went to the sunlight band one of them wore, which allowed exposure to daylight without harm. Her pride swelled a little. It was her most significant achievement, the one thing saving the coven.

What would the first vampires do if they were here?

That question haunted Jaqlyn day in and day out. She'd figured out a way to beat the terrible effects of the sunlight on vampires. Now it was time to conjure up a solution to ensure vampires could proliferate.

Jaqlyn went into her lab and experimented until the sun set had diminished above. It was quiet outside the lab; most of the coven had gone out to hunt. They kept the new births locked in the cellar below the lab. This was the time to discuss her theories with Jeoung.

She could barely recall the life she lived before she became the undead. Truthfully, she'd rather not remember, because during that part of her life she had been a piece of matter floating through the world in a thick haze, only assuming she existed. She remembered the joy she felt after her first hunt, and she shut her eyes in ecstasy.

The year was 1803, the beginning of the Napoleonic war between Britain and France. A gash of radiant light broke through the cauldron-black sky as blood spurted from the wounds of fallen warriors who wailed and screamed in pain. Those left standing stabbed their way through with bayonets and swords against the wall of the enemy under the moonless sky. France, the enemy army was much stronger than the British army. A storm of musket bullets whizzed through the air and landed in their midst, killing more soldiers.

Jaqlyn stood in the middle of it all, filled with despair. The British would lose the war if she didn't do something, but there seemed to be nothing she could do at that moment. A mere foot soldier, her destiny depended on the outcome of the war. If they lost the battle, she would lose her home forever, and her life would be over. Lost in thought, she did not see the fusillade as it shrilled through the sky. When one bullet hit her from the back, she groaned and fell on her knees, losing blood rapidly. She could only stare hopelessly and in fear of death.

Still, the battle raged on. A tempest of shouts and bayonets rasped and keened through the black sky even as a maelstrom of cannon fire whizzed and whistled. Then came a blast that took down the last of the soldiers on her side—fewer men screamed and screeched as the ground became slippery with sludge and the blood of their comrades. She watched them blubbering and choking as the battleground became slimy with intestines. The battlefield was a theater of destruction filled with the cries of terror and wet red-colored mud. After the last rounds of cannon fire, the enemies advanced on horses. The bones of the dead and dying broke and popped a sea of enemies trampled over them. All around them, the effluvium of death. The enemy made an easy meal of the British army

While waiting for death to come for her, Jaqlyn saw shoes approaching. They were not the shoes soldiers wore. When she saw his face—the chiseled perfection and the piercing red eyes that glowed even in the darkness—she refused to die before knowing what he was.

"There, there, child. You shall be reborn into something more glorious than you can ever imagine," he said.

With his sharp index fingernail, he tore into his wrist and fed her his blood. It was the first time she tasted blood. It was dry like tarnished metal mixed with sweat. There was the underlying iron taste, as if she sucked on a metal coin. As his blood coursed through her body, her wounds closed.

"Who are you? What did you do to me?" she asked when he eased away.

"I am Quillan, son of Shara the Witch."

"What? What did you—"

He shushed her, and with a quick twist of his hands, snapped her neck cutting her off mid-sentence.

When she awoke days later, the unfamiliar surroundings befuddled her senses. No longer on the battlefield, she couldn't tell whether or not she was alive. Quillan sat in the corner and watched the realization set in.

"What did you do to me?!" she screamed through a rasped throat.

"I killed you. Killed the human in you so an immortal vampire could be born. By feeding you my blood, I became your creator. I am your sire."

"What the hell! What did you do, what have you done?"

"Listen, that pang you're feeling inside you is hunger… hunger for human blood. You must either feed now or die for all eternity." He smiled, his eyes glowing vermillion red.

The fear settled deep inside Jaqlyn's heart at the reality of her situation. The hunger was intense. Her blood grew hotter, and it parched her throat more than ever.

She recalled the carnage from the battlefield. Quillan seemed to know what she was thinking. He grabbed two horses from their camp and led her back to the battlefield, scattered with dead men with mangled limbs. However, there were live soldiers there too, the wounded and the sick, hanging on to life. The battlefield was the perfect place for her first hunt, and so she did. She was an undead and famished.

4 | JAQLYN

THE COVEN HAD BEEN HOME to many generations of vampires, Zhovs and Gha'ueos alike, for more than a thousand years. The coven sat on an ample secluded space of land on the Scottish Highlands surrounded by acres of rolling plains and high mountains. The Zhovs restored the ruins of an unknown castle and made it their home, far away from all mortal humans.

Made of the most exquisite architecture, it had three moats, a steeple, and a dome-shaped stained rooftop. All the windows were stained and covered with heavy luxury curtains to keep out the sunlight. Every room appareled with antique furniture, and there was a damp cellar below ground where they kept most of their meals.

The tall dome loomed in front of her like a medieval castle. Amid the evening mist and the rising moon, the stone walls held a supernatural stillness. Reflected firelight illuminated the windows about five stories high, and Jaqlyn could see the other vampire's shadow cast against the pane of glass. Jeoung stood mindful over the coven-like he was the king. She had the impression he needed to be reminded he was not. He was beneath her, merely a leader, an ascendant, and a member of the council. On the other hand, she was the superior ascendant in charge of the coven and the head council member. Her authority well exceeded his.

The drawbridge that crossed the moat was slick with moss and algae, painting it an eerie green. The portcullis lowered but hovered two feet from the stone floor, a means of cautioning would-be intruders. Jaqlyn's torch reflected off the water of the moat, home to dark things that swam just out of sight. The courtyard beyond the gate was shaded except for a single fire brazier burning atop the ancient fountain. Its water absorbed all light as Jaqlyn crossed and walked into the dome, only to see Jeoung coming down the last flight of stairs.

All around her, newly turned vampires fed on weak humans who were captured solely for that purpose. The sweet smell of blood filled the air, but Jaqlyn sensed the blood could be much more delicious. The best blood was created with fear pulsating—a prey caught after for several minutes, thought they could escape.

Jaqlyn stared with disgust at the human bodies littering the floor. This was not what Shara the Witch intended when she created the undead. It was Jaqlyn's duty to lead the coven back to their glory days and the destiny they were meant to have. This dull and humiliating existence would not and could not continue.

5 | JAQLYN

"IT'S IMPOSSIBLE, JAQLYN. WE ARE the undead. There is no way we can reproduce," Jeoung said with a solemn expression after she finished her proposition. "The only way for vampires to multiply is to turn humans," he said with an air of superiority about him. Although second in charge, it was noticeably clear from his tone and mannerisms he wanted Jaqlyn's position.

"They are too weak to fight! Don't you see?" Jaqlyn responded. "If we don't do something drastic, we will become extinct in no time. You listen to me, Jeoung. No time at all!"

Jeoung folded his arms across his chest. He was appalled at the solution she proposed. Jaqlyn could tell what was going through his mind. He thought she was too stubborn and her idea was unrealistic and impracticable. But he was the one who would not get his head out of the clouds. They would become the last of the vampires if they did nothing. It was inevitable, and it irked her to no end she was the only one who could see the tragedy that would soon befall them all if things continued this way.

"You need to forget about this, Jaqlyn. Go back to your lab and focus on creating more of those sunlight bands for our newborn vampires. After all, they are what made you a wealthy vampire. But forget about that experiment. This is my last warning to you."

Jaqlyn watched Jeoung's eyes turn crimson. He bared his fangs in an obvious threat, and she hissed with a little bow. Two could play that game. She would not let his lack of foresight be the end of their kind, even if it meant taking matters into her hands.

Then and there she decided she would not allow this blind fool to detour her plans. She gave Jeoung an insincere, "Very well," before turning, leaving him without a chance to say another word.

This is the future he has in mind for us. These weaklings?

She made her way back to her large laboratory. Before the war, and before she was turned, she had obtained a degree in biology but always had a fascination for the darker side of science. She paused at the entrance and stared proudly at the magnificent archway. She went all out in the design to create the look of a place with great achievements.

She walked to her primary lab, situated down a short hall. The brightly-lit room had multiple crystal-covered lights that hung from the ceiling. The metallic-looking black floors were smooth. Jaqlyn's lab was orderly and clean. She had developed a system for organizing everything, and no one was allowed to touch anything without her permission. A large metal shelf held research equipment and tools. Toward the back of the room, tubes, and wires running across the floor to and from power sources, monitors, and other important-looking equipment flowing with energy.

The walls were lined with many bottles filled with liquids, powders, pills, human parts, and tissue. Behind the closet door were more shelves holding apothecary jars, specimens, and science books—everything was in order, labeled, and color-coded. There was one exam table near the north-facing wall where one could see the sky through the dome above. The walls painted with renditions of former Vampire Elders, also known as the grand elders and great elders—the most powerful of their kind—now dead by the hands of humans. The laboratory had made her a wealthy woman indeed, but now it was time to pursue loftier dreams of saving her coven and her kind.

She did not need Jeoung's permission, and at this point, she no longer wanted it. She was not going to wait for him or the other council members to admit the importance of what she was attempting to accomplish. She would have to take this journey alone. She knew in her heart that Shara would pridefully approve of what she was trying to do. Creatures as magnificent as vampires should not die out just like that. They were the more powerful beings, and to survive, they had to fight back.

They had known the secret for years, despite their powers and abilities, they had a terminal weakness. It was not supposed to get out, and if it hadn't, they would still dominate the earth and every creature inhabiting it.

Humans believed their weakness was silver, and for as long as she could remember, vampires let them believe it.

With a silver blade in hand, the humans were convinced they were safe and could not be. It kept them docile, and the vampires chose to let them wallow in the false safety of their stupid myths. The truth was silver certainly had a peculiar effect on vampires, but it was more like the effect sedatives had on humans.

The vampires' true mortal weakness was a rare mineral that was never spoken of. It was what had killed their creator, Shara the Witch, and her son, Quillan. For eons, the knowledge had been kept a secret among the highest order of vampires and the Gha'ueos, the elite bodyguards of the coven. The Gha'ueos were a deadly lot with years of training that translated into abilities that weren't seen amongst regular vampires. No other bloodsucker, except for the order they guarded, could match their speed, strength, and ferocity. Everyone feared them.

Of all the vampires in the Zhov's coven, the most formidable was the seven council members. A mixed-race considered the law, the jury, the judge, and the executioners who oversaw the entire coven.

Then there was Jeoung, an Asian vampire who had been part of the coven since 1862 when Shara turned him. When Shara found him, Jeoung was a revolutionary severely injured after trying to escape during the Muslim rebellion in Western China.

Contrarily, Jaqlyn was a Zhov and council member who knew the secret they had all sworn to keep for the rest of their immortal lives. As long as that secret was not common knowledge, they would be safe, and their position in the food chain would remain unchallenged.

Nevertheless, humans had discovered the rare mineral and its detrimental effect on vampires. She knew what her next line of action would be, but first, Jaqlyn would convene with the other council members in hopes of getting them to see the brilliance of her plan. She would not let Jeoung lord over her. It was time to start a revolution of her own.

6 | JAQLYN

"NO, IT IS NOT THE time for a revolution, Jaqlyn," Jeoung spat. "Are you insane?"

Jaqlyn felt her anger rise like waves in a raging ocean. She couldn't tell whether they were mad or just blind.

"Can you not see what is going on? Someone out there knows our secret, and they are killing us off in hordes." The council members in the room gasped aloud, and Jaqlyn felt disgusted at their ignorance. These were matters they were supposed to know, being leaders of the coven.

Continuing to drive her point, she stated, "Are you not tired of hiding? First, we hid from the sun, and now we hide from these spineless humans. They know about it—they know about the 67th element! We are headed toward extinction! Shall we stay hidden and wait for them to hunt us down one by one? My plan is the last hope we have!"

After she finished, she looked at the council and saw them stare back at her as if she were mad. What she proposed was unheard of, but surely they knew of Jaqlyn's brilliance since she had created sunlight bands that protected them against the destructive effects of the sun. But they found what she suggested to be blasphemous.

"Jaqlyn…" Jeoung drawled in a condescending voice that never failed to make her furious. She stared at him from the center of the room with distastefulness displayed in her eyes.

"What you suggest cannot be done."

"Oh, but it can be done! I am the only scientist in the room, and I know what I am saying!" She was losing her temper, so she took several deep breaths to calm herself.

"Yes, child, calm down," Jeoung said.

Jaqlyn growled in response. She hated it when he referred to her as a child because she knew he used the word solely to destabilize and belittle her in front of the other council members.

"Zhovs, fellow council members," Jaqlyn repeated when she was once again in control of her emotions. "Humans know about Holmium and know how to make weapons with it!"

She studied the faces in the room and felt her hopes plummet. They were not listening to her; they all spoke amongst themselves. She knew they would side with Jeoung. Besides, they could not imagine bringing her idea to life because they thought it would diminish their purity. They didn't want to know and didn't bother to question her. How was it any different from what they were already doing by turning witless and weak humans into witless and infirm vampires? She couldn't comprehend it.

"Jeoung has told us of a plan, a *good* plan, to put an end to the new threat the humans pose," Cathelyna spoke slowly in a grating voice. She was a woman of reason and the only other female council member of the Zhovs. "It is not as drastic a plan as what you are suggesting, Jaqlyn. Your plan is too volatile. There are a million things that could go wrong with it. How can you not see that?"

Jaqlyn shut her eyes.

Not you, Cathelyna. Not you too…

If there were one council member sure to back her idea, it was Cathelyna. Now, as she stared into this other woman's violet eyes, Jaqlyn's plans withered. She felt alone—but she was determined to make them see reason.

"There is nothing drastic about my proposal. Why do *you* not see that?"

"Any attempt to create vampires through any means other than the traditional one is obviously drastic and should not be considered by anyone. Least of all you. This meeting is over," Jeoung declared.

Jaqlyn saw it in his eyes—the sense of victory mixed with a healthy dose of "Fuck you, Jaqlyn." This was no longer about saving their coven. No, it was well beyond that for Jeoung. For him, it was about exerting his dominance over her. He wanted to show her he was a leader, their leader, capable of making sound executive decisions.

It was a moronic power struggle. What disgusted and offended Jaqlyn more was realizing that the other members of the order—vampires supposed to be the wisest on earth—could not see through his façade. They also couldn't appreciate the critical flaw of their survival strategy: weak humans could only make weak vampires.

7 | KALLISTA

THE AIR OUTSIDE HER CASTLE rock home had an arctic feel to it. Perhaps it was the biting cold of the winter fast settling in, or maybe it was the cold inside her body manifesting itself as the weather. She couldn't tell either way. Whatever it was, Kallista knew she didn't like it—she had always preferred warm temperatures to cold ones, even though it didn't benefit her. Her vampire blood would always overshadow the human in her. She scoffed. *Human blood! Ha! What a joke!*

You're unique, Kallista.

The words reverberated in her mind as she recalled her mom, Jaqlyn. Jaqlyn the Dark was what the members of the coven had named her. Her mother often reminisced about being a fierce vampire in her prime, one of the best fighters her coven had ever known. Someone they used to worship…until they stopped.

They will hail you, Kallista. They will love you or pretend to. Until you make a mistake. That's when they turn on you. That's when you truly realize that you have no friends.

Those were her mother's favorite words. She recalled the bitterness in Jaqlyn's coal-black eyes every time she uttered them. Kallista had hoped her mother would one day try to reassure her it wasn't her fault. Reassure her that she was not the cause of her mother's misery. But Jaqlyn never did—no words of comfort came from her lips. Jaqlyn was her trainer, her mentor, her boss; she had been everything but a mother. Whenever it was convenient, Jaqlyn reminded Kallista that she was her mistake, what alienated her from her people.

"It doesn't matter now," Kallista whispered to herself as she stared at her reflection in her bedroom window. "That belongs in the past."

For a long time, she had complained about being different. She realized she was not like the other kids, and she wished she could have been. She had vampire blood in her, making her half-undead, half-human, and an albino. That made all the difference in the world. Jaqlyn's words still echoed in her mind.

You will learn to forget the human in you. You are made of me, made of my essence. That's more important than anything your weakling of a father might have left in you.

Kallista pulled a red sequined dress from the closet and rubbed her hand over it in a serene gesture. It was at total odds with her heritage. She winced as her mother's voice continued resonating in her head. She tried to block the sound, but it was not working.

Why was Jaqlyn's voice in her head at all? She had been free of her mother's presence for several decades. Now was not the time to backslide. She had to get ready for the night. She had to find a new mark.

Kallista paused for a few minutes before deciding where she would go. She grabbed a robe off the door hook and wrapped it around her body, gazing at the full-length mirror on the wall. There was a definite advantage to having good looks. Many men had told her she was the most beautiful creature they had ever seen. Like moths to a flame, they were drawn to her. It was not her fault they kept getting burnt to crisps. She had made a meal of all of them without compunction.

"You're so beautiful…"

"You're perfect…"

"Please marry me…"

"I'll take care of you…"

If she had been human, she might have fallen for the sweet talk and dashing looks these men had to offer. From men with abundant charisma and charm to those who were challenging and even the annoyingly overconfident and arrogant ones. She wasn't a regular human. She was Kallista, one-of-a-kind.

Her hair streamed down her neck in a wave of Nordic white ringlets, and when the sun hit it at the right angle, it would light up in such brightness that all shaded their eyes to avoid being blinded. Now and again, her hair would change into something else—a mix of blonde and silver when the need to feed was not severe, but amber-red when feeding or in battle. The color could also turn to the whitest of silver when she had not fed for a long time—that was when her true nature came out to play.

Commitment, family, love… none of these words held meaning with Kallista. She had all the time in the world, and nothing else mattered. She had no family ties and no mortal emotions. She was not tethered by the things that repressed humans. All she cared about was living and surviving. After all, she wasn't a regular human.

8 | JAQLYN

JAQLYN STARED AROUND THE COUNCIL chambers in one last desperate move. She hated being perceived as desperate; it made her angry. Anger and desperation were a volatile mix with the potential to explode, leaving a trail of destruction in their wake. The members filed out of the dome-shaped chamber, leaving Jaqlyn alone. She gazed at the sky through the transparent roof and struggled not to scream.

Holmium, the 67th element, was the most horrifying discovery of the Zhovs' existence. When they stumbled on and read the old notes left behind by Shara, they had been thrown into an abyss of unrest and strange emotions. They felt something they had no idea they were capable of feeling—fear.

Shara had been killed by one of those closest to her using a blade forged with the rare element. For years, it had been unclear how Shara had died. One day, they stumbled upon Shara's diary, which had detailed information on how she created vampires, but more importantly, their one weakness—Holmium.

After Shara created the first vampire, she had attempted to turn herself into one of her creations. It would have been her key to untapped powers and becoming the immortal she had always wanted to be. But, despite her efforts, she had been incapable of going through with the process. To create the undead, she had to die, and there was no one she trusted enough to manage the process with the same precision that only she could achieve. She attempted to cast a spell on herself to become immortal, but it did not work the way she had anticipated. She gained more strength than the average human and a ravenous appetite for blood—but she did not entirely become a vampire, and it left her vulnerable to the same weaknesses as her creation.

Her apprentice, Ransley, was the only man who knew about her weakness. When Shara's appetite grew so ravenous she ended up killing Ransley's only son, she successfully set the stage that led to her death. Filled with rage, Ransley set out to forge a weapon with Holmium, and when the time was right, he plunged it into Shara's heart.

Jaqlyn sat in council chambers reading Shara's notes memorialized on the parchment she had discovered a century ago. It contained Ransley's confessions of killing her and details of the blade he had used. There were rumors of another diary detailing how Ransley had plotted the witch's death, but no one ever found it.

The Zhovs were aware of how rare the element was, but they also knew that a drop of Holmium in human blood was all that would take to bring an end to the vampire unfortunate enough to feed on such a human.

They had protected this secret for a long time, but now, that secret was out. The humans knew about it, but how? And they were using it to eliminate vampires en masse. It did not look like the genocide would stop anytime soon. The coven felt it was Jaqlyn's duty as a head council member to put a stop to their extinction.

She was a vampire-witch—she would do as she pleased.

With just a slight variation on Shara's spell, Jaqlyn would create a new breed of vampires immune to Holmium.

"The first creation of mixed-breed vampires shall be mine!" Jaqlyn said.

For the spell to work, the human in question had to be willing, and Jaqlyn prided herself on being the best seductress. Humans were, and always would be, predictable and easily manipulated. But, secretly, they had something for which she longed—the ability to procreate. She would procreate, and when the Zhovs saw the result, they would have no choice but to realize that a mix of vampires and humans was not an abomination or taboo—it would be their saving grace, their future.

A bell rang out in the distance and Jaqlyn dashed out of the coven. She recognized the pealing sound as the emergency alert. Another vampire had been killed. In her hundred years as a vampire, Jaqlyn had heard the bell ring more times that month than she had in the previous ninety-nine years. When the killings started, she had been curious to know the cause of death, but now the curiosity was transformed into an urge to act. She had to find a robust human male to use in her plan. And soon.

As Jaqlyn turned to walk back inside the coven, Laylen caught her by surprise as he too had rushed outside at the sound of the bell.

"Why won't the Zhovs do something about this? Why do we let these witless humans hunt us down? We are the predators, and they are the prey. Or has that changed?" Laylen asked.

She turned to Laylen with a glacial expression as they walked into the lab and shut the door.

"Jeoung thinks the only way we can get out of this is to create more vampires. We know our killers are a group of humans, but we cannot attack them because they know our weakness. They hold the tool to our destruction. But I will have my way."

"You're absolutely right. Creating more vampires is of no consequence. Not when Holmium kills them too," Laylen agreed.

"Exactly! That's what I told them, but they want to play it safe. The irony!" She slammed her palm down on the metal lab table, causing a slight dent. "Vampires wanting to tread the safe path. Never thought I would see the day!"

He had been her myrmidon apprentice since she changed him from a human into a vampire of her own one hundred years ago. It was the era of World War I and the Russian Revolution, the year 1917. He was a soldier gutted and left to die. She remembered walking on the body-littered battlefield, looking for food. It had been a long time since she had had a satisfying drink, and nothing tasted as good as fear-spiked blood. She knew humans feared death, especially when helpless, when stripped of their defenses, and when there were no friends around to assure them that all would be well. That evening, she had quenched her thirst after a long drought.

"Stupid humans!" she had griped as she walked over their bodies in her blood-soaked white dress. She loved wearing white whenever she went hunting. There was something about the crimson on white fabric that sent chills of fear down the spines of humans.

She could only imagine the horror she had inspired in the men as they watched her approach them—a beautiful, deadly woman with bloodstained hands, bared fangs, and burning amber eyes like an erupting volcano.

Each of them screamed as she bit into their necks, but soon they would experience something akin to peak pleasure as she drank their life forces.

Everyone except Laylen was terrified. There was no fear in his eyes, even in that terrible circumstance. "I have been waiting for you," he managed to say as she stood over him and blood rose from his throat.

There was something about this soldier's courage that moved her, so she decided he deserved a second chance at life. His inner strength was dignified and vampire-like.

Then, she knelt beside him and lifted his head to the crook of her arm as it fell limp to one side. In his neck, she saw the shallow pulsating artery. She sunk her fangs into his neck and drank just enough to change him. Today, Laylen was the most loyal worker she had.

"So, what do we do now? Do we put a hold on your plan?" Laylen's eyes widened with uncertainty. He knew Jaqlyn had a stubborn streak in her, but they both understood that going against the Zhovs was to court a permanent exile from the coven.

"No, we proceed as planned. This is our last hope."

Laylen bowed and headed toward the box in the corner to unlock it. Jaqlyn joined him, and they both stared at the man inside.

The male human had been selected by Jaqlyn herself, picked out of a select group of men as the perfect human to give her what she wanted. He was good-looking and had the air of a leader about him. Smooth, toned brown skin, a testament to his African origins. Other soldiers of his unit seemed to look to him for direction. The man had the strength needed to see the ritual through, which was critically important. A face like a god was an added advantage.

To Jaqlyn, he was perfect. She wanted an alpha male for this experiment. "If we're going to mix their blood with ours, then it has to be the best we can find, right?"

The man's fingers twitched, which meant the sedative Laylen had given him was wearing off.

"He'll soon wake," Laylen said.

"Take him to my bedroom chambers. Keep him out of sight from the coven. Strap him to the bed," Jaqlyn commanded. "I'll meet you there."

Laylen did as he was told, easing the box containing the man along the corridors of the coven remaining unseen. Once inside Jaqlyn's bedchambers, he took the man to the bed and strapped him down. Jaqlyn entered the room right behind him. Laylen then stared at Jaqlyn, awaiting further orders.

"You may leave now," she said in a hushed tone as she shooed him off.

It was time to set the stage. The ritual needed a relaxed atmosphere, one conducive to seduction.

She closed her eyes, and that was all it took. Her powers had grown exponentially over the years. All she had to do was picture what she wanted to see, and it happened in the blink of an eye. Gone were the times when she had to cast spells to get such mundane things to happen.

She wore a scarlet red gown, and the plunging neckline was just deep enough to show the right amount of skin. Candles were lit all over the room, emanating a subtle scent of jasmine into the air. The spell for creation had been perfected, and the moon was high in the night sky, which meant her time was near.

9 | JAQLYN

AS HER CAPTIVE BEGAN TO wake, Jaqlyn carefully undid his straps one by one and backed away from the bed to put distance between them.

"Who are you?" the man asked in a hoarse voice.

"They call me Jaqlyn," she said with a brilliant smile. He was the sacrificial lamb, and in this case, fear was not required. He had to be at peace for the spell to work.

"You're absolutely captivating," he slurred as he took in her glistening brown skin and her thick black hair flowing around her face.

Her job was already half done. "And you are breathtakingly handsome."

She could see the look of gray metallic ores in his eyes, signifying the spell was still in place.

"How did I come to be here? This is not my home," he said in a panicked tone, still under the haze of the spell.

"No, it is mine."

"How did I come to be here?" he asked once more.

"You don't remember? How we met?"

"No, I don't…"

She smiled and put in his head memories of him meeting her in a meadow just outside of town, false impressions of attraction and blazing lust. Then she watched his pupils dilate, glorified with admiration.

"Oh, how could I forget!" he said as if he suddenly remembered. "I'm a fool to have forgotten you." He rose to his feet, and Jaqlyn sauntered toward him in steps designed to seduce.

"No, you're not. You're a man. It is the way of men to forget things after a while. The world is full of captivating souls."

"None as much as you," he whispered.

His eyes were heavy with desire, and Jaqlyn felt herself responding to him. He was an attractive man, and she was a woman with passions that blazed.

Their bodies brushed against each other in a dance as old as time. Jaqlyn's eyes changed from her usual dark color to amber, just as it happened when she was on a hunt.

This was a hunt, she supposed, but it was different hunting—it was a hunt for survival. She would still derive a great deal of pleasure from it.

His mouth hovered near hers as she wrapped her arms around his neck, his breathing labored as she felt her magic at work. Science had played little part in what she was about to do. While it had given her the idea of procreation, to actualize it, she needed magic. She needed to go against the laws of science. To create life from an assimilation of the undead and the living would require the help of dark magic.

He moaned as his lips brushed against hers. Jaqlyn met him with a fervor burning brightly, both lost in a tornado of lust. With the first kiss, their souls intertwined, and Jaqlyn began chanting her spell in silence. She had all she needed—a man, her mind, and the lust pulsating in the air like a living being.

Jaqlyn felt a tingling sensation, liquid pleasure pooling from the base of her head all the way to the core of her womanhood. This man whose name she did not know, whose eyes burned with the flames of lust he did not really feel, was igniting fires for her that went beyond the spell. When his arms snaked around her waist, she paused and let herself be taken by him. When he entered her, her eyes rolled backward. It was an unusual feeling, unlike any she'd experienced before. She had always been the one to take, seducing men with calculated precision, then saving her thirst for after sating her lust.

"You're amazing." He took a deep breath and then, went back to ravishing her body. He crashed upon Jaqlyn like a tidal wave slamming upon a shore. She loved every minute. Jaqlyn had not imagined that the lust would be so powerful, so intense. This was more than her spell at work. She felt as if she were bonding with the human, and it made her a little anxious.

She relished the moment as the spell took form in her mind. It rolled through her head until there was no space left for anything else. She cast the ritual in an ancient language, only spoken by a few. Words found in the Latin book of spells that had belonged to Shara the Witch. Shara's spell of Immortality was the key to unlimited power and possibilities. Once she unlocked that, she knew she could achieve what had been possible in her mind only once.

Their souls were intertwined at the core, and the spell moved from Jaqlyn's mind to ancient and guttural words that were nothing like the human had ever heard before. She became lost in the power of the magic as he reached his climax. She called all the forces of life, "*Planto mihi ago insquequo vicis subsist,*" and felt her dead ovaries fill with life. Minutes after he had orgasmed, she felt the instant the human's sperm and her egg fused together. Her spell had worked—she had created the first living vampire. A vampire who would not be susceptible to Holmium or any weapon fashioned from it. A vampire who would be unaffected by the sun. All her years of research and perseverance had finally paid off.

The words rolled out of her mouth, and the ground shook in testament to the new life forming inside her womb.

10 | HENRY

SUDDENLY, HENRY FROWNED AND GLANCED around, although he was not sure why.

"Something is going on… What are you doing to me?"

The woman who rode him mindlessly paid no mind to him. He watched her mouth move without pausing for even a single breath of air. As he kept watching, glimpses of his identity flashed in his head until he finally remembered who he was. One thing was clear to him— he should not have been there.

Something awful was happening to him. The more he stared, the more he saw that the woman having sex with him, not a woman at all. She was a monster… She was what he had been born to kill: a vampire.

"No!" he screamed. "Get off me! Now!"

She continued, unbothered. The man could feel the power of her legs wrapped around him. He should have lost his arousal, turned flaccid, now that he realized what she was, but his body betrayed him. His eyes kept gravitating to her luscious breasts, and he felt his senses feast on something he could not name. Another incredible sensation he did not recognize tore through his entire body; it too was a delicious feeling. It took him a moment, but then he realized what was happening.

She's killing me.

"I said get off me, you godforsaken creature!"

"Yes, God has forsaken my kind. And now he has forsaken you too!"

Then her eyes turned an amber-red, and her fangs came out to play.

As she continued taking advantage of him, he felt dirty, like the lowest scum on earth. He screamed out in frustration. He realized with a great deal of shame that, even though he remembered his identity and knew the woman above him was not human, his cock remained rock hard, and his body wanted nothing more than for her to continue sliding up and down on his penis. The memories of where he had been a few hours before came back to him.

His last recollection before being in this room was addressing his followers in the Grimoir sanctuary—they were the most devoted to the Grimoir beliefs.

"I am the direct descendant of the man who ended the reign of one of the evilest beings to walk the surface of the earth!" he had shouted in the sanctuary. "My father Jason Grimor, his father before him, and all my ancestors have gathered resources for this moment!"

The crowd shuffled when he paused to drag in a much-needed breath. Excitement filled the air, and they were all aware of how much was at stake. Theirs was a sacred group, and the time was finally right to make their move.

There were weapons all over the room, from daggers to knives to swooping blades. Their mission was simple: to rid the earth of the vermin that walked upon it—vampires.

For years, his ancestors had been forging weapons from the substance in the sacred mine, but they had no idea why they were doing it. His father, Jason had told him the story of his deceased father before. That story had passed down for generations along with a single hint that made no sense until they discovered the log of Ransley Grimoir.

CREATE WEAPONS FROM THE MINE AS IF YOUR LIVES DEPEND ON IT BECAUSE, IN THE END, IT IS ALL THAT WILL SAVE YOU.

They were the words of his ancestor, Ransley Grimoir, and it was the last thing he said to his young grandson Jason before he died. Upon hearing those words, Jason Grimoir grew up and created an elite cult of vampire hunters. Before his death, Ransley Grimoir was a sorcerer, and he taught his grandson what he could. But magic is an art. Some people have a head for it while others just don't, no matter how hard they tried. Jason Grimoir did not have a head for magic. Ransley's workshop had been secretly built on the sacred Holmium mine. Unfortunately, things weren't that easy. Something was missing…

To create a proper vampire-killing weapon that could be used by a human, it had to be infused with magic. Otherwise, the vampire would overpower the human before they even got to use it.

Ransley Grimoir had learned magic because he had the natural talent for it. Born a magician, learning sorcery had only been a way to hone his skills. His grandson, Jason had to wait until someone in his lineage had the same natural talent as his grandfather. The same ability his father had before the witch had murdered him. Ransley was the only person trusted to infuse the weapons with magic.

They waited years before he was born. He, Henry Grimoir, was supposed to give the Grimoir cult a purpose and end everything. He would revolutionize the dying cult by recruiting new members and infusing the weapons created over the years with the magic to make the Grimoir cult a formidable army.

We had come so close.

Now, trapped beneath the thrusting body of a vampire, he looked at the monstrous woman above him. He watched her lower her fangs toward him, and he closed his eyes in despair. But he couldn't give up now. The force of her magic tied his tongue, which only allowed him to communicate in muted tones.

He felt a momentary pain when the fangs broke the skin on his neck and buried deep inside his arteries. He felt his head grow light as the pleasure increased. It was sickening, but it was also beautiful. He felt tears touch his cheeks as the vampire moaned from his blood coating her mouth. He now remembered how she had captured him and realized she didn't even know who he was. If she did, he would be in the dome of Zhovs, not on her bed. He would be tortured until he told them everything he knew. He would have stood no chance. They would have done everything possible to break his spirit and everything that held his soul together. He would have been condemned to eternal damnation and become a total disgrace to the Grimoirs and the cult his family had built for generations.

Perhaps it is better this way.

His people were getting ready for another attack. The plan was already in place, and regardless of his circumstances, he knew what he had to do. It was his job as the leader to ensure his followers had a solid idea to work with. If there was any lesson he had learned over the years, it was that they would be lost without a solid plan. He had read Ransley Grimoir's log and had become familiar with the weaknesses and strengths of vampires. He also knew that they had more strengths than weaknesses and that it would take a solid plan to get rid of them the way he had in mind.

He created his plan painstakingly, and the rules were simple—always have the advantage of surprise, do not let them see you coming, never get captured, and die before you allow that to happen. It was ironic that he, the leader of the group and the one who made plans, had gotten captured.

The Grimoirs didn't see them coming. His people were right in the middle of the meeting when the two men—or so they thought—appeared. That was the first time a vampire had attacked them, and they were not prepared for it. They carried no weapons and stood no chance. He even tried to cast the simple magic he knew, but the vampires were creatures of magic as well. The short spell was deflected, and before he knew it, he had fallen into what he now realized was a sleeping spell.

Moments later, he had woken up with this woman.

"You are so beautiful," he tried to say. He was getting weaker, and the words did not come out.

There was an explosion of pain as he felt himself fading away. Then, darkness.

11 | JAQLYN

JAQLYN REALIZED SHE HAD NEVER asked his name.

He dies beneath her, and she staggered off his body and closed her eyes to absorb all the power broiling within her. It was a success. She carried life inside her. The joy made her weep in delight.

She would have a child, the first vampire to be born and not created. There was no way the Zhovs would punish her now. Instead, they would celebrate her, and her name would go down in history as the first vampire to achieve what even Shara the Witch could not.

Wild laughter escaped her mouth, and she continued until she ran out of breath.

"Blasphemy!"

"I can't believe she would do that!"

"She has created a monster!"

"She must be punished!"

Jaqlyn stared at the council members, seething with anger. She could not believe they did not see the benefit of what she tried to accomplish. How could the council not understand that she was trying to save them? How could they all be so blind? It was beyond her understanding.

The noise reverberated around her, but she disregarded it. She had given life to a being that others had said was impossible, and now it was growing within her. The vampires' bewildered expressions at what she had done did not look like they would subside soon. Left to her nemesis, Jeoung, he would have killed her right there and then.

As the banter continued, Jaqlyn could not take it any longer and screamed, "Enough!" The sheer force of the power in her voice silenced everyone.

"I will have my say," she started.

"What do you have to say for yourself?" Jeoung asked with contempt dripping from his voice.

12 | JEOUNG

HE DESPISED THE SIGHT OF her before him. She carried inside her something that was at odds with all he had ever held dear. A pregnant vampire was unheard of. Jeoung couldn't help but wonder why she was so hell-bent on upsetting the status quo. He was convinced there was no way humans could wipe them all out. If they stuck to the plan of changing humans to vampires, they could never go extinct. Aided by his Gha'ueos, he made a significant discovery about the sudden increase in vampire deaths in the past few weeks. Other information he got would change the whole narrative and turn it around in their favor. But he kept that information to himself because of an epiphany he had.

A wise man once said to him, *Chaos is a ladder.*

It was time to put that saying to proper use. If Jeoung could single-handedly end the vampire killings, he could show the others he was the right vampire to lead the coven. Once in a position of power, he would become the most influential and powerful vampire in the entire world.

Jeoung cast his mind back to the day he made his discovery. He had been with the Gha'ueos when they came across a vampire pursuing a human.

Jeoung was hunting, and the other vampire had been doing the same. The vampire had caught up with his prey, and Jeoung believed it was only a matter of time before the vampire drained the human and moved along. But something unexpected happened. With a flash of hand, too fast for any human, the human produced a blade from the folds of his winter coat and buried it in the vampire's heart. He recalled the gasps of horror from his Gha'ueos as they watched the vampire's skin fall off and turn to ash.

"What the fuck?" one Gha'ueos blurted.

Like him, the journeymen Gha'ueos fighters had been trained to deal with things like this their entire lives. They had learned too much about Holmium not to recognize it at work. However, unlike his newly-turned Gha'ueos, they did not understand what they just witnessed.

There was something different about that human. He looked up to see them watching him and turned around to escape. In a flash, the Gha'ueos matched his speed and were soon beside him. The human managed to kill one of the Gha'ueos before the other two disarmed and captured him.

Only one Holmium blade was known to be in existence, and it was kept out of sight of the Zhovs. Jeoung assured it was locked away in the dome, and it looked nothing like the weapon the human acquired.

He used his skills as an expert torturer to elicit answers from the human. Even though the human had been unwavering, Jeoung eventually got the answers he wanted out of him. When Jeoung finished making him talk, the human was bleeding from head to toe.

The information Jeoung had gotten from the human was vital. Jeoung learned there was an ancient order of humans dedicated to ending vampires. It was the most ludicrous thing he ever heard, but he also knew their knowledge of Holmium made them dangerous.

What he should have done was meet with the Zhovs and formulate a strategy to end the ancient order of the humans. This would have resolved it, but he had another idea in mind.

"Tell no one of this," he had told his Gha'ueos.

No one would know of this, not unless he decided it was time for them to know. He had his plans, ambitious ones, and the chaos the humans were bound to unleash would catapult him to the heights he wanted to achieve. Jaqlyn was the only person who could derail his plans. He had to get rid of her, and the only way he knew how was by discrediting her in front of the entire coven—especially the Zhovs.

Jeoung looked down at her from his position and smiled to himself. She had made the whole thing easy for him. Even he could not believe she would be so brash. She had dug her own grave, and now it was time for him to bury her in its depths. He would push for the death penalty, but before then, he had to get everyone in the coven on his side.

"My people!" he said in a voice that traveled around the room. Everyone went quiet as they listened to what he had to say. "I made a discovery that will put an end to these killings. You see, Jaqlyn was wrong to have thought her way was the only way. I have a better way. And my way is the way! Simple and straightforward!"

Jeoung saw the rage build in Jaqlyn at the realization that her plan was not going as expected. Not only had the coven not embraced her idea and effort, but the likelihood of any admiration or celebration for her pregnancy was also bleak.

"I speak the truth," Jeoung said with a look of triumph as he stood among the coven. "I have put together an elite group of Gha'ueos who are now on their way to the hideout of the humans responsible for the killings within the past months. I ordered them to kill on sight. The humans have been staging attacks targeting small groups of vampires. I saw fit to put an end to them before they attacked the coven."

"But how is that possible? Humans killing vampires. How did they get the Holmium?" asked a voice from the coven.

"They discovered an ancient log written in the words of Ransley Grimoir that contained an account of how Shara's apprentice killed her and a description of the source of the 67th element."

13 | JAQLYN

THE ROOM FELL INTO ABSOLUTE SILENCE. Rage, disappointment, and the echoes of Jaqlyn's failure could be felt around the room. It was over for her. What she had done was not necessary, at least not with enough urgency to get the Zhovs to consider it. It was no longer their only option. The danger was no longer as imminent as Jaqlyn had imagined.

She looked up at Jeoung and understood power dynamics. She knew at that moment, in that room, he had won.

He sneered, and the rage multiplied within her.

"When did you make this discovery, Jeoung?" she asked through clenched teeth.

"Recently, but I only confirmed it yesterday. The cult is led by a man called Henry Grimoir, and so far, they are the only ones who know about our weakness to Holmium…"

Jeoung continued his explanation, but Jaqlyn was no longer listening. There was a dull ache in the space where her heart should be, but dimly, she realized she must have been imagining the emotion.

So, this is what loss and defeat feel like?

She had never experienced either before. Her body shook, and her breathing accelerated. As she refocused her attention to Jeoung again, she heard him say, "What you have done is unheard of, and you will pay for it with your life."

"Surely death is too severe a punishment," said Cathelyna.

Jaqlyn stood in the middle of the room without uttering a single word. She might have lost, but there was no way she would stay and let Jeoung end her life and the life of the child she carried.

She had not learned Shara's language only to die. She started chanting. The power arose within her, and she could see the amusement on the faces of the entire coven, but Jaqlyn did not stop. A violent gray aura surrounded her as she turned to walk out of the room.

"Stop her!" Jeoung screamed at the Gha'ueos in the room, but none of them seemed willing to touch her. She had been elevated to a dimension none could reach, as if a swirling wall protected her.

"Stop it, Jaqlyn! You won't die here today!" Cathelyna interjected with displeasure.

Jaqlyn looked around her. Perhaps there was a chance.

She stopped chanting, and the atmosphere went back to normal. If Jeoung tried to murder her, she vowed to turn the whole place to dust.

14 | LAYLEN

KALLISTA OPENED THE DOOR AND saw it was Laylen. She turned and walked away without a second look. "What do you want now?"

"I've been calling you all week," Laylen said.

"I know. I chose not to answer your calls because I do not want to see you. I didn't want to see you then, and I don't want to see you now."

"When will you forgive your mother?" Laylen asked with his face twisted with worry.

"She is not my *mother*. She told me that more times than I can count. She has never been a mother to me. Did she send you here? Don't answer that—of course, she didn't. So, why do you insist on building bridges where none can be built? Why? I don't understand, but it doesn't matter. Just get out of my house and don't come back."

Kallista said the words in a flippant tone with no emotion. There was no anger and no heated expression, only plain disinterest.

Laylen knew there would be no redemption for him. But if he gave Jaqlyn what she wanted, he could find peace from the guilt he carried for decades. He had hoped by now Jaqlyn would have forgiven him and trusted him again, but she hadn't. He was desperate to get Kallista to return to the coven, her home. If not, there would be hell to pay.

"If you insist," he grumbled, but he lingered still. In a flash, Kallista twisted around with her unique and unmatchable speed. He felt the sharp pain in his forearm and stared absentmindedly. For a moment, he could not think or breathe. He watched the skin fall off where she nicked him with the Holmium blade.

"Get out, or the next time, I'd plunge it in your heart!"

That was motivation enough to skedaddle. Kallista hated him, and so did her mother. He was done, at least for the moment. He had no desire to become a dead vampire. It had never come to this in the past. Kallista threatened him with the one thing that could kill him, and he was terrified to no end. He could see he had pissed her off and this wasn't his intention. It was best if he left while he was still alive.

She stood with her back toward him, and in silent acquiescence he retreated her home the same way he had entered. It was time for a new strategy. His life depended on it. Perhaps it was time to give up his chase of a reunion between mother and daughter.

As Laylen paced outside Kallista's home clenching and unclenching his fist in frustration afraid to react, he concocted a new plan. He was anxious and felt like a failure—two feelings that now felt like second nature. Laylen was also fearful of returning to Jaqlyn with the news that her daughter refused to come home.

All she will see is that I have failed her once again.

The thought left a bitter taste in his mouth. He had to feed to get rid of it.

Nervous of what would come after telling his boss he'd failed, Laylen felt his mouth become dry as he entered the laboratory. Jaqlyn swiftly pinned him down with her cold, dark eyes.

"Tell me you found her," Jaqlyn demanded.

He winced. "Yes, I did. But——"

The words stopped mid-sentence as she continued to stare at him.

"But what?" she said as her eyes blazed.

"Yes, I found her. She's in Castle Rock, Colorado. But Kallista would not listen to anything I had to say, Jaqlyn. In fact, she sliced me with a Holmium blade." He knew Jaqlyn would be just as perplexed as he had been to hear that news.

With a look of outrage on her face, Jaqlyn asked, "Kallista has the Holmium blade? How is that possible? How is she using it? How long has she had it?" Jaqlyn had so many questions.

"If I may…" He inhaled deeply in a last attempt to put his new plan in motion.

"What is it?"

"I think you should meet with Kallista yourself."

He felt his heart hammering against his chest even as he said the words. It had been years since mother and daughter had spoken to each other. But he believed it would go a long way in turning things around.

"See Kallista?" she asked softly while peering at nothing in particular.

"Yes. Maybe you can reason with Kallista, make her see why she is needed back here at the coven."

"She won't listen to anyone, the arrogant twat! It may be a clever idea to make this trip on my own. All she does is play games with humans when she could be here training at my side."

Laylen stood stiff with uneasiness but smiled tightly. For the umpteenth time, he wondered when he could make Jaqlyn see that he was loyal to her. Surely, she had to see that he was doing his best to prove himself. Now that Jeoung was gone, thanks to Kallista, Jaqlyn was once again the most powerful vampire around. Apart from his debt of loyalty to her, he also wanted to be in her good graces. He would do whatever he had to do to regain her trust.

"Just let me know what you need taken care of," he said. "I promise you it'll be done."

Her eyes shifted across the room, and he felt the contempt she harbored for him was fast disappearing. However, his relationship with Jaqlyn still hung on by the last threads.

15 | KALLISTA

DOWN IN THE NIGHTLIFE DISTRICT of Denver on the first floor of the church nightclub, Kallista gazed over the heads of the crowd in search of her next prey. The humans in the club were out to have an enjoyable time, and so was she. She observed the sea of bodies gyrating on the floor, arms wrapped around one another, moving to the loud pop music blaring over the speakers. On any other night she would be out there dancing, but not tonight.

She could feel it all, their most basic instincts and desires. She knew what she wanted, and for her to get it, she had to look into their heads. Her eyes roamed from one man to the next, looking for a handsome specimen in need of company. It couldn't be just any man—he also had to be more than capable of catering to all of her needs and pangs of hunger.

Too many emotions slammed into her mind in that busy place, which was the reason she preferred to block out the crowd. Feeling and listening to their thoughts was to understand their pain. She would rather listen to their joys and happiness. By understanding their pain, she could grasp their mundane worries. And she was not interested in any of that. Just as the thought occurred to her, a wave of pain washed over her, and she pinpointed the source: a lone woman sitting at the bar nursing what looked like her fifth shot of brandy.

Should have never gone out with that asshole. God, I'm so stupid!

Kallista sighed. Women and their silly emotions. Humans knew nothing other than how to cause each other pain.

Another voice intruded. *I should ask her to dance, or maybe talk to her friend first…*

She looked at the man in the corner, fixated on a pair of women on the dance floor. Her eyes traveled over him, and she discarded him at once. Besides, he had no penny to his name—at least not enough to do what she would need him to do.

She tried to block out the feelings of the people on the dance floor, but it became difficult the longer she stayed. Humans were a pretentious race, and there was a lot of hidden pain in the club that night. Beneath all the drinking, music, over-heightened conversations, and dancing, they were just little children hiding and running away from their real issues. Their thoughts and emotions felt less like words, and more like thrusts of sharp needles stabbing her. They were like multiple porcupine spikes piercing, causing her intense pain.

However, Kallista was stronger than they were.

She continued to focus on the men in the club, especially those who looked like they were at the club alone. This was not the best place to go for a hunt, but it was the place she had easy access to that night. All she needed was one lonely man who would welcome her attention, somebody looking for something new. Someone who could take care of her needs. She stayed on the upper-level floor of the club and let her eyes roam the room.

After about half an hour, she saw an older gentleman at the bar trying to mingle. She not only got a strong sense he was lonely, but she could also see he was a wealthy man.

He stood about six feet tall and wore a suit that Kallista estimated to be worth at least five thousand dollars, and the watch strapped to his wrist was a Cartier. He projected the aura of wealth, and Kallista knew he was the one.

She walked down the stairs in a move designed to catch the attention of the room. She wore a short gold dress that accentuated her hair. It was a simple dress, but it showed off her curves advantageously. Her calves were encased in strappy black high-heeled sandals that made her legs look like they were a mile long. Men turned around to look at her, and women turned their noses up at her.

She read their thoughts.

Damn, who are you?

I'd love to be balls deep in you.

Who does she think she is with her gold minidress?

Kallista walked across the dance floor, letting her mark's feelings guide her straight to him. The man rocked slightly to the music, and he gazed directly at her as she walked over and stopped beside him.

Kallista unleashed one of her most charming smiles. Her exquisite looks and the club's dim lighting made her silver eyes enthralling. She knew she was irresistible and always used it to her advantage.

Come dance with me.

She moved her lips but sent the thought to his mind. He would believe she had spoken, but he could not have heard her over the roaring music blaring from the speakers.

The man looked at her, then looked around the club, confused. Kallista listened to his thoughts. He wondered why a woman as exquisite as her would ask him to dance.

"Dance with me," she mouthed again as she stretched out her arm and wiggled her fingers. He found the act coy, so he nodded and reached for her fingers. She felt elated as she led him to the dance floor. She could see he was a little shy, but that didn't matter because he was welcoming all the same. Snaking one arm around her waist and the other around her shoulder, he drew her close. With a twinkle in her eyes, Kallista smiled at his boldness with acceptance. She was a foot shorter than him, and her head only reached his chest.

Falling into the rhythm of the music, Kallista moved her body close against his as she began to twist and turn. She molded to him in moves designed to be sexual. She enjoyed the way he felt against her body, and as they danced, she realized that underneath his suit, he was masculine, with well-defined muscles for a man of his age. It was the hardness she found attractive in her men. It was clear he enjoyed the feel of her warm body rubbing against him through her skimpy clothes.

As they danced, she felt his cock rise, tenting his fancy pants, and this pleased her. The music changed to one with a faster pace, and so did Kallista's moves. They danced and flirted with their eyes, thighs brushing and loins grinding. She could hear the man's heart beating loudly and knew he was now hers.

Surrounded by a crowd of writhing bodies, assailed by their emotions, the pressure in her head increased at a rapid pace. Though the stabbing pain in her heart intensified, she focused on him. The only reason their feelings and thoughts affected her so much was that she had not fed in a while, and her vampire senses were heightened. Her pain would ultimately dictate her actions.

She fought not to succumb to its demands for as long as she could. She looked up at the man she danced with and tried to ignore the emotions. The music changed to an upbeat rock selection that Kallista did not like. The man slowed and stared at her. He was a little breathless.

"You are stunning," he said when he finally found his voice. Kallista batted her eyelashes and sidled up to him.

She analyzed his looks and concluded he wasn't handsome in the way she preferred her men to be. He had a fascinating face, but she preferred sharp angles and masculine lines on her men. He had an almost pretty, feminine look. His gray eyes were intense, which were appealing, barring that he was also courteous and obviously wealthy. Kallista wetted her lips suggestively and looked up at him. He wanted her badly, and she knew he would agree to her terms. Willingness was all she needed.

"I want to be alone with you," she whispered into his ear, inhaling the smell of his cologne and sweat. She closed her eyes as she drew it in, and she made sure he saw that she desired him. He took in a deep breath and smiled at her. She knew what she wanted—a bit of blood and a lot of semen.

Let's get out of here, she suggested to him, telepathically so. There was no resistance, only a smile that expressed something bordering on worship. With his hand on her lower back, he led her through the crowd. She let him think he was in charge, that he was the one who had just picked up a beautiful woman in a bar and was now taking her home. As they walked through the crowded club, Kallista sensed the random emotions around her.

A stranger's envy tore through her.

How did he get that beautiful woman to follow him home? How? What a hottie!

Kallista was satisfied with what she heard from the stranger and let her eyes run over him. While she had naturally captured his lust, tonight was not his night. He did not look wealthy, and he acted like a loser. With his jealousy, she decided he would have been an easy mark. She winked at him as they passed him, flashing a smile.

Get over yourself.

He stared at her. He had heard the words but hadn't seen her lips move.

Yes, ponder on that.

She smiled at him again and let her catch guide her out of the club.

All the emotions that invaded her headspace that night increased her hunger. In a few minutes, she would feel better. Her chest rose in anticipation as she inhaled. She couldn't wait to have him. She telepathized this to him, and he quickened his stride, steering her through the side exit.

16 | KALLISTA

SOON THEY WERE IN AN ALLEY. It was quiet and dark with boxes stacked at various heights on one side. Kallista scanned the area to make sure they were alone. She spotted a homeless man at an entrance going through some trash.

Leave now. She commanded with her mind the homeless man. She waited as he shuffled out of view. Then she moved up to the gray-haired man, pulling him into the corner behind the boxes.

"You're fascinating," he said with a slight accent. Kallista wondered how she could have missed it.

"I know," she replied with a coy grin. There was no way he was getting away. She turned him around so she was against the wall and he caged her in.

"What do you want from me?" he asked.

"I want you to kiss me," she said as she encircled her lips with her tongue, tilting his head down to hers. "Your lips are so luscious."

A delighted look broke out on his face as she said the compliment—compliments always worked. There was no resistance when her lips met his. He opened his mouth around hers, searing them in a demanding kiss. His tongue slid through her parted lips and tangled with hers within seconds.

"Stop," she whispered. He did as asked and stared at her through eyes heavy with desire. Now she had him. It was time to feed.

His lips glistened from the kiss and, at that moment, he looked handsome to her. There was something about his vulnerability that amused her. Kallista brushed her hair away from her face and eyed his neck. She could see his vein pulsing with blood. There was no stopping her. She was never supposed to feed on men who were meant to take care of her. She fed on those who had nothing to lose. But her hunger yearned, and it demanded to be sated, immediately. It was calling to her like a beacon of light from the lighthouse guiding a lost sailor home. Her lips touched the skin of his penis before her tongue darted out to lick him there.

He wailed, letting out sounds at odds with his masculinity. Kallista was happy to hear it.

"Come home with me," he whispered to her.

While Kallista appreciated his invitation, she did not intend to accept it. What she wanted was something else entirely—a little of his blood to get rid of the pallor of her albino skin. She would go hunting later that night for a full meal, but for now, she needed something to quench her thirst. His vein beat against her lips, a movement so subtle a human would barely notice it, but her senses were supernatural.

Her fangs lengthened, pushing past her lips, and in the darkness, the man could not see them—nor could he see her Nordic white hair turn amber red. He was too lost in the pool of lust to pay attention to anything other than the feel of the woman he held in his arms.

"Let me take something from you," Kallista said. The man felt the warmth of her breath in a low, hushed tone.

"Anything you want," he replied, dazed by attraction.

The sharp tips of her fangs sank into his neck and broke through the skin. She sensed the fear suffusing him as he felt the brief pain. Turning around, she pinned him to the wall in a swift move. For a split-second, he struggled against her, but her arms imprisoned him. She hauled her body into his, crushing her breasts against his chest, and willed him to be at ease.

Relax.

His body went limp, and his blood streamed into her mouth. Her skin changed to the color that flattered her most. Her silver eyes transformed into blood-orange, and her body felt alive.

She heard the man moan as she fed on him. His cock, deflated when she pierced his skin with her fangs, sprung back to life. She caught the wave of lust that emanated from him, and with a pleasing look, she smirked. Then, he was at his most vulnerable, and his thoughts came pouring out toward her.

God! I want to bury myself in her slick heat!

Kallista eased away from him. That thought was her wake up call. He grew weak, his breathing went shallow. She checked to see if she had done real damage, but she hadn't taken much of his blood.

Her skin regained its youthfulness and the hunger subsided, she released his neck and licked the puncture wounds. Her saliva closed the two small holes instantly. Come morning, there would be no visible trace of her feeding on him and no side effects.

She had to ensure he had no recollection of what happened in the alley. She looked into his eyes and sent thoughts into his mind.

Nothing happened here. We were never in this alley. We left the club and went straight to your car.

17 | GEORGE

TOGETHER, THEY WALKED BACK INTO the club through the side exit and took the main door out. His black Mercedes was waiting for him, complete with a chauffeur who sprang into action as he saw George approaching.

"Ready to go home, sir?"

"Yes, but first, we'll take this beautiful woman wherever she wants to go."

"Hello," she said to the chauffeur, and George was struck once again by how sophisticated she sounded. He stared at her and smiled to himself. He was utterly smitten.

She smiled up at him and told him her address. The chauffeur opened the door, and they slid into the back seat.

"I'm George Hanson," he said finally.

"Kallista," she replied.

"Kallista what?"

"Just Kallista."

"That's interesting. So, Kallista, I would love it if we could go on an actual date tomorrow."

"It would be my pleasure, George."

They smiled at each other and spent the rest of the trip basking in each other's presence.

He walked her to her door and placed a chaste kiss on her cheek. He wished he had dared to kiss her properly, but it was his way of being a gentleman. "Pick you up at seven tomorrow?"

"Yes, that sounds good," she said, whispering into his ear as they hugged. The hug felt like déjà vu, pleasing, almost as if he had embraced her somewhere before. He expected her body would feel soft under his hands, and he was pleasantly unsurprised.

That was when he was convinced that meeting her wasn't happenstance. He'd met the love of his life.

She is the one.

Something about the woman fascinated George, and he was excited by the prospect of spending more time with this mysteriously beautiful woman. Tomorrow could not come soon enough.

18 | JEOUNG

JEOUNG CALLED A SIT DOWN with all the council members and other notable members of the coven. Based on rank, the members sat around the big table. Since none of them was of age to become an elder, Jeoung and Jaqlyn, being the two highest-ranking nobles, led the coven until a new elder was selected. It had been many years since the last elder was murdered. Jeoung sat at the head of the table with Jaqlyn seated opposite him, though she was next in line to become an elder. The five other low-ranking noble council members sat around the table at the other end while the commoners stood around the perimeter of the room. They'd congregated for a meeting to determine Jaqlyn's fate and how to move forward with coven matters.

"We should kill her!" Jeoung thundered. He was drunk with the power he now wielded over the others.

His Gha'ueos had returned, and he knew they had fantastic news. "My lord!" one of them said on entering the meeting room.

Jeoung smiled when he heard his head Gha'ueos. Finally, everything was going according to plan. "Yes, Desmond. Tell me the great news."

"We stormed the human's hideout in the early hours with the ancient weapon you gave us, blew their walls open, and found them inside. There were forty men, and they were not expecting us. Although we lost ten vampires, the cult is now gone. There will be no more vampire killings."

Jeoung watched the fury light up in Jaqlyn's eyes, and his smile intensified. Jeoung relished knowing everything was coming along nicely. He could not have planned it better.

"I'd like to know why we are only just hearing about this plan after it has been executed," Cathelyna said. "Why didn't you inform the council before sending out your Gha'ueos? You are not a single leader. You are part of a council. Care to explain yourself?"

Jeoung pursed his lips together. He had to choose his words carefully, or his plan might crumble down around him like a house of cards. He turned toward the silver-haired vampire with a smile fixed on his face.

"Yes, Cathelyna, that is indeed a very valid question." Eyes were on him from every corner of the room, but he was nothing if not a master of lies. They would not see him flinch. "I made this discovery only a few days ago, and I did not want to bring the information to you until I confirmed it to be true. My Gha'ueos went prepared because Holmium is a formidable threat and they had to defend themselves if needed."

Jeoung's answer did not explain why his Gha'ueos went with a bomb created by Jaqlyn. He could see Jaqlyn tilting her head to one side, strongly indicative of a challenge to his response.

19 | JAQLYN

JEOUNG WAS PLAYING GAMES, AND that mush was obvious to Jaqlyn. The others were too bemused by him having saved them from extinction to see who he really was and what he was up to. She could see it all, but she would bide her time until the perfect opportunity for revenge presented itself.

"You just happened to have taken the most powerful weapon in our arsenal for a scouting mission by your personal guards and the newly turned vampires?" Jaqlyn said in an undertone.

"Yes, I did," Jeoung replied. "Because I had the foresight to understand that a group of murderers with enough Holmium to kill scores of our own must not be treated with kid gloves."

He raised his hands like a messiah and looked around the room. The other nobles bowed their heads in a show of acquiescence to his explanation. Jaqlyn shut her eyes at their stupidity. Perhaps she was the only one who understood Jeoung well enough to see through him. He had known about the human cult for a long time, and he'd kept it to himself while waiting for her to make a mistake that would discredit her and leave the path to power unchallenged for him.

Jeoung turned to her, leaving his back exposed to the other members of the council. He winked at her, and she saw triumph infusing in his eyes. He was mocking her, and he wasn't hiding it.

A smile broke out on her face because she now knew what she had to do: she had to kill Jeoung. "You will meet your end from my hand. I promise you."

She did not realize she had spoken the words aloud until the room went silent. The faces of the council members in the room expressed shock.

"Jaqlyn went against the clear order of this sacrosanct room," Jeoung said, seizing the moment. "She created something she might not be able to control. She has changed the face of order as we know it, and if we allow this to stand, we may as well open our doors to chaos and entropy."

"Yes, yes… You have spoken well. What do we do?" William asked. He was a little vampire with a deceptively soft voice, but those who know the name William often looked around with fear when he was in their vicinity. His strength was unlike any other vampire. His small stature had been the end of the creatures he fought with in the past. Underestimating William meant signing your own death warrant.

Jaqlyn knew he was not on her side. He was a stickler for the old ways, and she expected to find no sympathy from him.

She stood and moved to the middle of the room with her head held high as she stared into the faces of her judges.

This is not the day I die. Not today.

She had a plan, and if their judgment did not go her way, she would rain hail and brimstone on all of them.

"Banishment," Cathelyna said. "I do not think her actions are vile enough to deserve death from the Holmium blade. Banishment is fair enough, and it delivers a strong message to anyone who would think to disobey the council. Even if that person is one of our own."

The other four Zhovs nodded in agreement while Jeoung stared at them incredulously. They outnumbered him, so he could do nothing but agree with their suggestion. Left to him, Jaqlyn would have met her demise that evening.

"Well, then. Whatever the council says is the final word," Jeoung said. "Jaqlyn Ilichova, you have flouted the rules of this coven, and I hereby banish you. You are to leave with your life and the clothes on your back. The contents of your laboratory and every other thing you gathered as a member of this coven are to be left behind. Otherwise, you will pay with your life. You have relinquished your right to have Gha'ueos. They are no longer yours to order. You have been stripped of your position as a member of the council of Zhovs. Now, be gone."

Jeoung motioned to his Gha'ueos to take Jaqlyn out of the coven. Her time there was over.

Ilichova.

The name reverberated all over the walls that caged Jaqlyn's memory of a time she had all but forgotten. Ilichova was her human father's name. It was a name known only to a select few, and she knew Jeoung used it to remind her that, once again, she was not a full-fledged vampire. Creation of a witch. She had been stripped of all she was, all she had built, and for what? For trying to help her people survive the next century and beyond.

The Gha'ueos who took her out of the coven knew better than to drag her. They knew of her abilities. She could tear them all to pieces without so much as flinching.

The sun was high in the sky when they stopped at the edge of the clearing where they were to leave her. She stood with her back to the coven and the Gha'ueos that escorted her. She told both Gha'ueos that if they came with her, she would make them head guards. They wouldn't have to endure Jeoung's unfavorable demands. Each accepted out of fear or loyalty and left with her to start a new life.

Jaqlyn would not look back. None of them would look back. That was her promise. But she also promised that this was not the last they heard of Jaqlyn Ilichova. Their day of reckoning would come.

20 | JAQLYN

"THEY BELONG TO MY PAST NOW," Jaqlyn said as she cradled her belly. Her unique child was growing rapidly. Her fight was not over—it was only just beginning, and she would not let this banishment stop her.

She looked up at the sun, it would soon set. She had to find shelter, but most importantly, she needed to feed. She had traveled many miles, and her craving for blood wasn't making her think straight.

Jaqlyn and her two Gha'ueos traveled for eleven days heading Southwest of the Scottish Highlands. Jaqlyn stopped at the foot of a mountain, trying to find shelter before giving birth. She sent her guards to climb to the top of the hill to see what lay on the other side.

One guard reported that there was a small village hidden behind a forest on the other side, and right on the river's edge stood about twenty houses.

"Then that's where we will go," said Jaqlyn said.

They hastened to the top of the mountain and through the trees to get to the other side. There was no time to waste.

She knew the danger of bloodlust better than any other vampire. If she did not feed soon, she would go on an uncontrollable killing spree that would attract far too much attention. On a typical day, she would have about nine hours before the bloodlust took over, but with the creature she was carrying, she did not have so much time. It was too early to tell the effect the child would have on her, but by her estimates, she had between two to three hours to feed, or the village she was heading for would suffer her rage.

Unfortunately, she was mistaken. The bloodlust came over her within the next hour, and it was unlike any she had ever experienced. She could feel her blood boiling and her head pounding. The urge to tear into someone's throat and feed until the victim's eyes lost all color was overwhelming. There was no point in fighting the bloodlust, so she embraced it with careless abandon. It was like a newborn baby, screaming and demanding until its wishes had been met. There was no will, no thought, nothing except the burning need to feed.

She burst into the village at breakneck speed. Her bloodlust had doubled the usual. There was no one in sight. It was quiet, and the two narrow roads were empty. The sign that hung over the entry into the village said *Ploctaw Village*.

The houses were small but built on firm foundations. They stretched out across the land between two gravel roads and were painted white with brown straw rooftops, close to the river's edge.

Her fangs were elongated, and her flaming amber-red eyes were blind to any form of empathy. She could hear only the pounding of blood pumping in her victims' blood vessels. She started with those hidden in the village tavern and stables. She went from person to person, tearing into necks, ripping throats out, and leaving a trail of destruction in her wake. Those who were lucky enough to be in their houses when Jaqlyn Ilichova came calling stayed in and kept their doors locked, praying hard for a miracle, for salvation.

They received none.

By morning, Jaqlyn's hunger had been sated. She stood now in the middle of the village, covered with the drying blood of her victims, surrounded by their bodies, feeling more alive and freer than ever. When she put a hand on her belly, it was twice the size it was the previous day.

"Accelerated growth," she murmured to herself. It didn't make sense that the hybrid child she carried would grow at a rapid pace. *Everything will be just fine*, she thought.

She took in a deep breath and opened her arms to embrace her newfound freedom. Although Jeoung had defeated her, she was alive and free. Now she could do what she had always wanted—lead her own lair. She would do what must be done to get where she needed to be.

Those in the village who had escaped her carnage considered her a monster. They were right. She was a monster, and she was about to change their lives as they knew it.

"Come out, come out, everyone! Come one, come all!" she shouted, but no one responded. She didn't really expect them to. "Oh, you children do not understand who you are dealing with," she called in a more authoritative tone. She was an expert at entrancing humans. It was one of her unique gifts.

"Everyone come out now!" This time when she spoke, she spoke to be obeyed. It was a command not to be refused. The remaining villagers walked out of the safety of their homes on shaky legs even though their minds protested. They had no choice but to respond to the command of Jaqlyn Ilichova.

The villagers confused and rendered speechless by this pregnant woman standing before them shouting commands. Jaqlyn saw the hate on their faces and laughed at their foolishness. They thought they loved their pathetic human lives, but all of that would change once she gave them the gift of immortality. They would thank her once she turned them into majestic vampires, into creatures of the night that had no fear of death.

She regarded them, and from what she could gather, some of them wouldn't survive the change. Therefore, she selected the strongest for the change and would keep the weak as food for her new vampire family.

Jaqlyn selected the young and the strong. She went for women of childbearing age and those who looked like they had valor in their eyes. Her army would need fortitude to achieve her goal.

"Who among you are persons of science or healers? Raise your hand now," she asked using compulsion, as she separated the grain from the chaff.

She needed a new assistant. One woman raised her hand. She looked frail and old, but Jaqlyn figured she would have to do. It was her lucky day because she was one of the ones she'd kept as food.

It was time to move on to the next stage. The process would drain Jaqlyn, but she had no choice. For any chance of survival, it was something she had to do. She made it fast, drained their blood while they stood—under compulsion—like mindless robots. After their hearts stopped, she fed her blood to them.

She changed twenty humans that day, and when they woke up ravenous with a hunger for blood, they did not care who or what their meals were—boys fed on their frail old fathers, and a young wife dug her new fangs into her disabled husband's neck, drinking from him until he was dead. They were all lost in their lust for blood and every human looked nothing other than food.

For Jaqlyn, it was the most beautiful sight she had seen in ages. It was the start of her new army. As her thoughts drifted back to those who had banished her from her home, she silently reaffirmed her vow.

You will all beg for your lives when the time comes.

21 | JAQLYN

JAQLYN STARED AT HER GROWING BELLY. It had been three months since they banished her from the coven, and she was grateful it happened. Her army was growing fast with the aid of the two loyal Gha'ueos guards. While it was nothing compared to the old coven's army, it wasn't what she was striving for at the moment. She had another vision for her lair, and that was all she could see.

In the three months since she turned the first batch of humans, they were already halfway through the process of building her a new lab. It was rigorous work to carry a child and oversee the progress of her lair. The pregnancy and building an army drained her energy. She struggled to make sunlight bands for all her vampires. Her attempts to produce enough of them made her so tired that she stopped altogether and waited until after childbirth to produce more. She could only create three bands, which she gave to Fariah—her midwife—and two vampires who served as her guards along with the Gha'ueos.

Without the bands, her vampires could only work at night and slept when the sun came up. It was a slow and frustrating process, but there was no other choice. The house she stayed had belonged to the wealthiest man in the village. He was not fortunate enough to make the list of people she had changed. Weakness was not allowed in her lair, and this man, despite all he had, didn't make the cut. He would have been a liability. Hers was a different time—one where money and affluence held no weight. Strength and survival instincts were all that mattered.

She sat at the edge of the bed and looked out through the window.

She felt a kick and placed a hand on her belly. She was close to full term. She would deliver soon.

"What else do you need me to do?" Fariah asked while sitting in a chair close to Jaqlyn's bed.

"Nothing—just sit. We might have to do this earlier than I thought."

An hour later, when the labor pains started, Jaqlyn felt pain so great it could only compare to when Quillan, the son of Shara, sank his fangs into her.

She had never given birth before, and she did not know what to expect with this pregnancy. It was merely a means to an end. She was trying to create something new, and her body was just the vessel to bring it to life. The waves of affliction seized her back as she laid on the bed and gasped. Only four months had passed since the night she performed the ritual that brought the hybrid child into existence.

The child was born that foggy night of September 6, 1923.

"What a beauty! And white hair." Fariah oohed and aahed. There was no doubt the child looked different, and with fascination, Jaqlyn realized that her pale skin was unlike any other she had seen.

"She is an albino, Jaqlyn," said Fariah in amazement. "A beautiful albino child."

When the child opened her eyes, Jaqlyn forgot all about her rare complexion in wonder. The child was gorgeous. Her eyes were a shimmering silver—an unusual eye color, one Jaqlyn had only heard about but never seen. A vampire with silver eyes would be more distinctive than any other. Then, Jaqlyn recalled something she had read a while back about vampires with silver eyes—they were also supposed to be the strongest vampires.

Only two other vampires in history had silver eyes. But there was no way to ascertain if their extraordinary strength had anything to do with the color of their eyes or if it was just a strange coincidence. One thing was clear though: there had never been another vampire with silver eyes aside from those two, not until the birth of this hybrid vampire.

"What will you call her?" Fariah asked.

Jaqlyn was startled by the question. She had never considered that the creature might need a name. "I don't know, and I don't really care."

She saw the thinly veiled surprise on Fariah's face. The child was only an experiment, and that was all there was to it. She felt no attachment, no motherly instincts. All she felt was a scientist's curiosity and a sense of wonder. She felt the same way she would have about any successful experiment.

"What do you think of the name Kallista?" Fariah asked.

"I don't care," Jaqlyn replied absentmindedly.

She could feel her body healing itself from the effects of childbirth. Her tissues and muscles were regenerating, and after a few hours, she was as good as new. It was now time to confirm if the experiment had indeed been successful. Fariah had washed the child and wrapped her in a blanket.

"Bring her to me," Jaqlyn commanded, the Holmium weapon in her gloved hand.

"What are you doing?" Fariah screamed with horror when she saw the blade. "She's a child!"

"Bring her to me, Fariah. She is my experiment. Now I must find out if my experiment was truly a success."

Fariah had no choice. She took the child and put her in Jaqlyn's arm gently. Jaqlyn looked down at the child's face, and after seeing her, she said, "She *is* beautiful. The most beautiful creature I have ever laid eyes on. She has goddess-like features she inherited from her father. Kallista, I think the name will suit you fine."

Fariah smiled briefly before watching Jaqlyn nick the child's arm with the Holmium blade. Blood oozed out of the cut. Jaqlyn watched with glee as the child's skin healed itself within the blink of an eye.

"I did it!"

It was three simple words, but it was a formal proclamation of success for an experiment that had cost her everything. It was also a signal that everything would be all right.

"I'll show you, Jeoung. You shouldn't have started this game with me."

Eighteen months later, the newborn child had grown exponentially. She was strong, fighting with vampires twice her size and twice her age. She needed to be trained.

No longer pregnant, Jaqlyn needed to take control of her new army, starting with the production of the sunlight bands. This was the real beginning of power for her, the actual origin of her redemption. And she intended to exploit it fully.

She established her lair and changed more vampires. Her new lab was finally completed, and she produced more sun bands, glasses, and weapons for her army. She tirelessly trained her stewards, including Kallista, to be the best. Obviously, Kallista beat them all. Kallista was better at everything. She had none of the weaknesses of regular vampires: she could walk in the sun and was immune to Holmium.

Jaqlyn observed that when Kallista was angered or needed to feed, she looked nothing like herself—she looked more like Jaqlyn. Her skin tone would darken, her eyes would become a fiery blood-orange, and her hair color would turn bright amber red.

Discovering that Kallista could also read minds caught Jaqlyn by surprise. She would develop her into the perfect weapon, a formidable one she would use when the time came for her to take back her rightful place in the coven.

Jaqlyn had a plan. She was the executioner, and Kallista was her ultimate weapon.

For a creature that was a half-human and half-vampire, Kallista fascinated Jaqlyn to no end. Jaqlyn didn't need Kallista for her next experiment, but she needed her blood to create hybrids immune to sunlight and Holmium. Kallista became Jaqlyn's obsession, and

Jaqlyn became increasingly focused on taking the experiment to a new level—creating a pureblooded vampire child from two vampires. Such a creature would have unlimited power. It was a challenge she'd attempted to solve for a long time without success. But things were much different now.

22 | KALLISTA

KALLISTA GLANCED AT HER FACE in the mirror. It had been a long time since she fed, and it was showing—her skin was sandalwood, her hair was linen gray, and her eyes became less luminous by the second. She knew what her body needed, and she should not have gone so long without feeding. Wrinkles were starting to appear, and there was nothing she detested more than looking aged.

The bedside phone rang, and she picked it up.

"Darling." The man's voice was husky with what she recognized as desire.

"Hello, George," she said in her sexiest voice.

"Oh, God, I need to see you again. Why do you run from me?"

"I'm not running from you, George. In fact, I'd love to see you today. I was just going to call you when the phone rang."

"Great minds think alike, huh?"

She could hear the pleasure in his voice, the thick sexual tension that awoke something deep inside her. What a shame she was almost done with George—he was one of the good ones. However, George was falling in love, which made him clingy and emotionally attached. Kallista was never in it for the long haul. She had one rule in the love-and-leave life she lived: leave no one alive. Such was her way.

"Where should I meet you? Same place?"

"Yes. Is 4 p.m. fine?"

"That's perfect. See you soon, darling," Kallista said as she hung up the phone. Her new mark would have to wait. For now, she would restore her beauty with George.

She did not want to risk getting so hungry that she would rip George's throat out, so it was best she found an appetizer to improve her appearance before meeting with him.

The woods behind her house were the perfect hunting ground. Animal blood would have to be enough for now. She touched the tip of her tongue to her fangs, feeling her mouth water. She imagined the hunt and felt a slight jolt of adrenaline spike through her body. She needed more blood than a small rodent could provide, so she would have to pursue a much larger animal.

She held up the dress she meant to wear that night but hung it back on the bedroom door and went to her closet for something more suitable for a hunt. The leather pants and fitted T-shirt were perfect because of their flexibility and durability. She grabbed her flat, non-patterned leather boots to wear. It was her preferred hunting gear, and when she wore it, she felt totally in control. Power sizzled just underneath her skin, then she opened her senses to everything she'd shut out.

The emotions hit her like a sack of rocks—the pain, the fear, the contentment, the joy, the disappointments, and the pursuit of food. Not only could she sense human feelings, but she also sensed those of every other creature. It was one of the banes and boons of having vampire DNA.

She had discovered the power when she was just five years old when Jaqlyn allowed her to play with the other kids.

I hate her so much, she heard someone say on the playground one day, and somehow, she knew the person was referring to her.

It hurt her that someone would say something like that about her. She looked around, trying to find out who was talking, but no one was. When her eyes clashed with Esme Monae's, she knew the words had come from her. The sun was high in the sky, and she was with the kids her mother had allowed to live so she could have a childhood. That was the only motherly thing Jaqlyn had done for her. But underneath it all, she knew she did not do it out of maternal concern. The real reason was simple enough—she was Jaqlyn's experiment, and Jaqlyn wanted to provide an optimal environment for development.

She recalled Esme Monae had been unattractive with the face of a walrus and ginger hair. Esme had blamed her and Jaqlyn for her parents' deaths, and she hated them for it. It did not matter to Kallista why the other girl felt that way because when she was grown, she would be turned into a vampire too. And she knew it. There was no escape for Esme. Her hate was wasted when, in time, she would become the same object of hate. Still, Kallista felt her hate and returned it with hatred of her own.

I hate you more, Esme Monae, she thought. Suddenly, Esme's eyes widened, and she looked away in fear. That was when Kallista knew that what she'd heard was not Esme Monae's words but her thoughts. She also realized she could put her own ideas in the other girl's head without speaking a word.

Later, she came to realize that she differed from every other creature on earth, and she hated that fact. She loathed being the only creature with unique abilities, never fitting in with any group. On the one hand, vampires hated what she represented. On the other hand, humans thought she was the weirdest thing they had ever seen. Soon, Kallista learned to keep her abilities to herself. Nobody cared about her, and if left to the vampires, she would not even exist. She would have been cut out of Jaqlyn's womb and killed before she could even take her first breath.

She was the first of her kind—a mix of human and witch with vampire DNA. Her pigmentation was that of an albino; the melatonin from the mixture of her parents' blood caused a reaction in her skin. Her body, her strength, her skills, and her intellectual mechanisms were so unique that nobody understood her for a long time, not even her own mother. But as she grew, she figured herself out.

There was no instruction manual in the world about how an albino hybrid was to live her life. She was on her own, and the world was hers to do as she pleased. Now, nothing would stop her from being who she wanted to be.

After returning from her hunt, she washed up and started getting dressed. As she did, she knew the time had come that George would be a problem, and she would have to close that chapter. Tonight, was that night. She put on her red dress and slipped her feet into her red Jimmy Choo Romy suede pumps with crystals. Then she brushed her hair, applied a light coating of lipstick, and dabbed perfume at the base of her throat and the sides of her ear, patting a generous amount on her cleavage. She looked in the mirror and admired how amazing she looked. She knew George would be so pleased.

23 | GEORGE

THERE WAS SOMETHING ABOUT HER that he did not fully understand. Perhaps it was her Albinism, her soft cream complexion, her silver eyes, her mysteriousness or the fact that she didn't talk much about her past that made him so crazy about her. Whatever it was, he was in love with her. She was not his usual type. She seemed fragile and innocent but with such a high degree of sexuality. All he wanted was for her to say yes to his proposal, so he could forever have her all to himself.

George Hanson stood on the balcony of his penthouse and looked out for her Aston Martin DB11. He had purchased the vehicle for her, not understanding how someone as stunning as her did not have a car of her own. He remembered her face the day he surprised her with the car. It had been glorious to watch her face light up with such joy and to know her happiness was because of him.

He soon saw her drive up and pull into the underground parking garage. He looked around the penthouse and smiled; it was perfect. He had even purchased two hundred roses to make this proposal special. They had been seeing each other for six months, and he could not believe how hard he had fallen for her. Yet he got the sinking feeling that Kallista was becoming disinterested in him.

He wanted her to be a part of his family. Nothing would make him happier. He had all the wealth and material possessions any person could want. But given his advancing age, the one thing missing from his life was a person with whom he could settle down.

"My God! We'll have such beautiful kids!" he said aloud to himself excitedly.

He then remembered his own parents and felt his mood plummet. He could not remember the last time they talked after a falling out with them many years back. His father was ruthless and tyrannical and only wanted a son who would obey everything he had to say. He'd always wanted George to take over at his company as the CEO, but George had no interest in the business of building boats and ships.

"That's what the Hanson family is known for, George. If you walk away from the family business, you are no longer welcome in this family," his father had said. He had a sister very much interested in the family trade, but his father would not listen. "Your sister will get married and have her own family. You are the man, and this is your birthright."

Such a sexist! George thought.

Managing that company would have been a disaster for him. He was sure his sister would excel at it. For following his dream as a computer software engineer, his father made him the black sheep of the family. It was unreasonable. He left home and came to America on his own. Since his trust fund belonged to him, there was nothing his father could do about it.

That was twenty-five years ago. George had become successful in his own right by building a worldwide mega IT company now worth millions of dollars. His father hadn't forgiven him, and he had been cut off from all the members of his family, all of whom were under his father's control. Everyone was forbidden to speak with him, at least until he came to his senses.

George missed his mother and sister, but they were so caught up in the web of his father's tyranny they had not contacted him in all these years. They also never responded to any of his calls or returned his emails. He continued to send them cards every Christmas, but after a while, he got tired of their attitude and stopped. What type of mother forgets about her son, even if her husband wanted her to?

He looked out and watched Kallista walk into the apartment building.

The night they first met would always be magical for George. That night, he was ever lonely and needed to be around people. Over the years, he had made many acquaintances but no real friends. It was not in his nature to make friends, because most of his life, he had directed his energies and efforts to drive his business. Now he was a highly successful businessman, his success had also made him somewhat socially inept in making friends. He would occasionally go out on a date, but he had not been involved with anyone because he was having difficulty meeting a woman he could stand for more than a few weeks. They all bored him after a while. His standards and expectations were too high.

So, when he was done with work for the day, he headed to the club. He had passed The Church nightclub a few times before, but that was his first time inside. He had hoped to meet a woman for a one-night stand to at least relieve his elevated sexual impulses.

That night at the club, he hadn't the courage to walk up to a stranger, so he went to the bar instead. He ordered a martini and decided that it would have to be enough for the night.

I'll finish this one drink and go home, he remembered saying to himself.

That was until he saw her. There was no leaving after that moment.

I think I fell in love with her that night. I stood no chance. She was everything I had been searching for. And now, she will be my family.

He had to marry her, and he needed to be the man she gave herself to wholeheartedly. All he wanted now was for her to say yes to his proposal.

Just then, the knob turned, and Kallista walked in. As always, since the night all those months ago, she took his breath away.

"Kallista, you look stunning!" he said, staring at her. "I was just reminiscing about the day we met."

"That was a long time ago, George," Kallista said in a quiet whisper.

"Not so long ago, my darling. It's only been six months." He smiled as he reached for her hand.

Kallista let George hold her hand.

The adoration and love in his eyes were visible. He drew her into his embrace that lasted longer than Kallista cared for, but she let him have that pleasure. On an average day, she blocked her mind to people's thoughts. But today, she had to know what George was thinking and how he felt about her. She did not want to end his life based on clinginess.

You're so beautiful. I hope you say yes. God, please! Let her say yes. Marry me, Kallista.

"I don't deserve you, George," she said to him.

"No, Kallista. I am the one who does not deserve you. You're so perfect, and I've missed you more than you can imagine. In fact, I have a surprise for you."

"I have one for you too, George." Her voice was husky with desire as she plastered her body to his. "I want to please you orally, George," she said with wide, innocent eyes, that had the brilliant silver color that fascinated him.

A broad smile broke over George's face. He let her push him back until he sat on the couch. Without saying another word, Kallista took two steps back and peeled her dress off her body in a striptease intended to increase his arousal.

George groaned when she bared her body before him. She was everything he had ever dreamed of and so much more.

Her skin was the smoothest he had ever seen, and from memory, he knew it was just as soft. How could he not want her to be his forever? She reached behind and unclasped her bra, exposing her breasts to his hungry eyes. They were perfect, perky, and topped with rosy pink nipples.

"My goodness!" he whispered to himself.

She continued to smile down at him as she noticed the outline of his cock underneath his trousers. He was already hard and ready. Unzipping his fly, she pulled out, wetted her lips, and ran her tongue up the girth of erection. He groaned in pleasure.

If there was one thing he knew he could never get with any other woman, it was Kallista's prowess at fellatio. After a brief period of teasing, he felt her wrap her mouth around him, taking his entire length in her mouth. She used saliva to make it pleasurable. Although it may have looked messy, to him, it was incredibly sexy.

As she continued, his moans became louder. But she didn't stop or even pause. She worked her mouth around him and gently cupped his balls in her hand, rubbing lightly. This heightened his pleasure, and he felt an orgasmic eruption spiraling deep inside him in no time. There was no use telling her he was coming. Although she was a virgin, he had not expected her to be so comfortable giving blowjobs or swallowing cum, but she seemed more than satisfied with it. She seemed to enjoy it, which was something else George found extremely erotic.

He could feel the waves washing through him as he reached his peak.

When he climaxed, he grabbed her head and held it to his cock straining to keep his thrusts gentle. Kallista opened her eyes and stared at George with his cock buried in her mouth and smiled. His orgasm had been so explosive he was struggling to catch his breath. But once it subsided, Kallista continued going. Breathlessly, he asked her to stop.

Kallista did not and would not stop. As she kept taking more of him into her mouth, her eyes took on an unhealthy and unnatural glow.

"Kallista! Stop!" He tried to pull her off him. George sensed something was terribly wrong. He had come already but could feel more semen erupting out of him into Kallista's mouth. The wave of pleasure intensified, but instead of welcoming it, it scared him witless. Whatever was happening at that moment, his instincts told him it was nothing good. After his second orgasm subsided, he said Kallista, "I need you to stop! Now!" But his voice no longer held the composure it had before—things had gotten weird. Kallista continued sucking.

He could feel his energy being drained and was losing himself even as he felt pleasure. A memory came rushing back to him. The night in the alley, he remembered the feel of her fangs tearing into his skin and pulling his blood into her mouth.

He now stared at her with horror. Her eyes were blood-orange. He begged. "Please… stop! Please!" Despite his pleas, Kallista did not stop. As she consumed every drop of semen he had in his body, his life force became weaker and weaker. He was only able to muster up enough strength to softly ask, "What are you?"

She had taken the last spurt of his semen, and his life was quickly fading. She pushed away from him and wiped her mouth. "Your end, darling. I am your end," she crooned.

George Hanson's last expression was that of horrified confusion. His final thought was the irony of dying from extreme pleasure. How fitting for a man who was a workaholic his entire life.

24 | JAQLYN

TWENTY YEARS AFTER JAQLYN'S EXILE, Laylen had finally found her. She had set up security unrivaled by any other, and he was captured as soon as he set foot across the set perimeter.

"My name is Laylen, and I've come to see Jaqlyn," he said as the guards created an impenetrable line of defense. It was unusual to have any vampire walking into their Ploctaw Village lair looking for Jaqlyn. He was told to wait there.

When the guard told Jaqlyn who was at the gate, she became furious. It was not in her to trust, but somehow, she had once come to believe in Laylen. She was not only his creator but also his mentor, and they shared a bond closer than a blood oath. Therefore, when she faced judgment in the dome of the Zhovs, she was confident he would be there right beside her, offering his support. But she had been mistaken, and she had learned a hard lesson.

No one was to be trusted, no matter how close they got or what promises they made. Trust should always remain a word and nothing more. Trust will kill you. Trust will destroy you.

As she continued to contemplate, she realized that she was alone in the world. There was no family, no love—only herself and the strength to survive. Those who were powerful and those who were powerless. Jaqlyn learned from experience it's always best to be the powerful, the ruler, the commander. Those were the ones people feared and respected.

They respect me because I hold their fates in my hand. The moment that changes, I am no more. I am no one. I must always be someone.

At her request, they brought Laylen to her. When he arrived, she made a conscious decision to stifle her anger. Brash emotions were for mere mortals, and she was not one of them. She was immortal. She was a vampire.

As he entered the room, she stared at him as if he meant nothing. He was merely someone from her past who, in her opinion, had shown his true self—a man devoid of loyalty. But before she could say anything, he dropped to his knees with an intense expression of regret written all over his face. It was more than clear to her he wanted to be taken back into the fold and relinquish his nomad's existence.

When he finally spoke, sensing her feeling, he said, "Forgive me, Jaqlyn. I was afraid. You were an elder, so I knew you would be spared. But I was a mere apprentice. Jeoung would have had my head on a stake. He wanted to make an example out of someone, and he wanted someone's blood. It would have been mine had I showed up. I had to save myself. I am terribly sorry."

Jaqlyn spoke no words. There was nothing to say. She knew what he was, but more importantly, she knew why he was back. Life was difficult for a vampire trying to strike it out on his own, especially for someone with Laylen's limited power.

"You are forgiven. You may return."

She uttered those words without emotion, making him no promises. Laylen was a vampire with experience in combat, and if there was one thing she needed, it was experienced fighters. Laylen was competent in both battle and politics. He could benefit her.

She watched the shock settle on his face but kept hers neutral.

"Really?" he said. Then he hastily cleared his throat and rose to his feet. "Thank you! You won't regret this!"

I know I won't, she thought.

25 | JEOUNG

MANY YEARS HAD PASSED, AND Jaqlyn's army grew larger and stronger. It became so much that news of its existence finally reached Jeoung.

"What do you mean she has her own lair?" he asked angrily. The Gha'ueos who brought the news stood in front of him without uttering another word.

It had been eighty plus years since the exile of the vampire scientist. In that time, many things had changed, but not for good. The Zhovs no longer had the power they used to. There was no order, nepotism was running the company, and anyone wise knew to stay on Jeoung's positive side.

The guard cast his eyes downward. Looking Jeoung in the eyes was to risk being deemed disrespectful, and nobody wanted to incur his wrath.

Jeoung rose from his seat, his body vibrating with restrained anger.

Jaqlyn is building an army for a specific reason. No one assembles an army for fun.

She was too power-hungry to stay in her new lair and be satisfied. They were cut from the same cloth, and Jeoung knew they both had ambitions that could not be quelled. She had declared a state of war, and only one coven would come out victorious. He would do anything to ensure his side won.

"I should have killed her when I had the chance," he muttered through clenched teeth.

The Gha'ueos who reported the update on Jaqlyn stood there awkwardly, too frightened to move as he waited to be dismissed.

"What the hell are you still doing here?" Jeoung asked.

The guard marched out as fast as he could.

He had to make a move and eliminate her and her army before she came for him. He knew Jaqlyn. She was not the type to forgive—she was the type to seize power.

Yes, that witch is coming for me.

26 | JAQLYN

"DID YOU TELL HIM?" ASKED JAQLYN.

"Yes, I did. Jeoung reacted exactly as you said he would. He's scared," said the Gha'ueos who had informed Jeoung of her growing army.

Jaqlyn let out a laugh of impending victory. She could feel it on her fingertips. She could smell it in the air. She knew how it would play out. Jeoung was nothing if not predictable. He had known all about the human cult and their Holmium weapon long before any other person, and long before he claimed he first found out. But instead of bringing it to the council, he'd kept it to himself and allowed vampires to be killed and did nothing, just to discredit her. He had dug the pit of his own downfall a long time ago, and she was now ready to push him in. The stage was set.

To win, one must know one's enemy. It was the first rule of war. It was a rule she had mastered, and one she knew better than most. Her real enemy was Jeoung. The other vampires on the council were pawns in his little game. He was the one she had to get rid of, and once done, everything else would fall into place.

The Gha'ueos had been captured by her men when they went on a reconnaissance mission. The day they brought the Gha'ueos to her lair, Jaqlyn recognized the rare opportunity for what it was. She had been planning for years, and finally, now was her chance.

"Don't touch them!" she'd told her men. If there was one thing she was sure of, it was that Jeoung knew how to misuse power better than anything else.

News of nepotism and disorder had reached her ears. Jeoung was running the castle like a spoiled child. The Zhovs had become powerless, and all the other vampires were tired. However, no one had the guts to stage a coup and send Jeoung to the pits of the hell, where he belonged.

Therefore, she pampered the leader of the Gha'ueos. Instead of treating him as a captive, he was a welcomed guest.

When they were alone, she asked him, "Do you know me?"

"You are Jaqlyn, the sorceress."

"I have developed a dislike for the word sorceress. I am a scientist. You see, magic can be explained if you have the mentality and drive to seek answers. My success has been based on finding answers to the many things that impact our kind. So, I would prefer to be called a *scientist.*"

The Gha'ueos stared at her. "If you're trying to convince me to join you, you don't have to try too hard. I will work for you."

Dressed in her signature black leather jumpsuit and low black quarter boots, Jaqlyn looked very much like a leader.

"That was a little too easy. Why should I trust you to be of assistance to me now?"

He smiled, but behind the smile, Jaqlyn saw pain and a story he wanted to tell.

"During the Holmium deaths, I lost my mate. She was everything to me, and she died by a Holmium blade wielded by an ordinary human."

Jaqlyn now gazed at him. She had never been in his shoes, but she understood him. She had seen vampires who wasted away after the death of their mates. It was the reason she swore she would never have a mate. She could not afford the weakness that came with having cared for someone. She did not want—and could not afford—to leave herself open to pain and have her spirit broken. Nevertheless, the pain of this Gha'ueos would open doors for her. She would help him channel his anger into something that would benefit them both.

"What would you do if I told you I know those responsible for your mate's death?"

He looked at her as if she were out of her mind. "I know them. It was the Grimoir cult led by Henry Grimoir," she said.

"I didn't know they had a name."

"They do." Jaqlyn stood up and poured herself a glass of wine. She loved the way the bittersweet liquid tasted. "Care for some?"

"No, thank you."

"As you wish."

Jaqlyn took a couple of slow sips, relishing each one.

"Your mate, did she die at the beginning or toward the end?"

"She was a Gha'ueos like me. She was part of a unit sent out to investigate the source of the Holmium murders. She never made it back with her unit."

"So, she died toward the end?"

"Yes. What are you getting at?"

"Your mate did not have to die. Jeoung knew about the Grimoir cult."

"The Grimoir cult," he said in a tone dangerously low.

"Yes. Jeoung knew about them before your mate was deployed, but he chose to let them kill his own kind to get rid of me. I had been advocating for the creation of a new and stronger vampire that was resistant to Holmium instead of just turning ordinary humans as he was doing. He knew I would be persistent and would go ahead with my experiment even though I did not have the council's backing. He waited patiently for me to make my move so I could be eliminated."

"I will do whatever you need me to do."

"Good. Who is your master?"

"Jeoung."

Jaqlyn was hardly ever surprised, but this news shocked her. Gha'ueos were meant to be loyal to their masters. It was one of the renowned qualities of the elite guards. "Why should I trust you when you are not loyal to him?"

"I care more about my people than I do my master. Jeoung is not doing a good job leading the coven. He has to go, and I believe you are the only one who has what it takes to overthrow him."

It was a simple enough reason.

"What is your name, Gha'ueos?"

"They call me Drake."

"Welcome to my lair, Drake."

The plan was now in action. The first part had been successfully executed. Now to kick-start the second part. One thing Jaqlyn had established was that, while Drake was one of Jeoung's Gha'ueos, he was not yet to be trusted. By giving him the news of her new army, she anticipated Jeoung would get together with his trusted Gha'ueos. That was the moment she meant to catch him and find a way for the rest of the coven to discover the truth.

Therefore, she did what she knew how to do best: she created.

To create a weapon, the target must be studied. The mechanics of the weapon must be fashioned to end the target's life. That was what Jaqlyn had done. She created a weapon that wasn't designed to destroy but collect data the most covert way possible.

She'd created a small video recording device, the first of its kind in the vampire world. It had been a while since she conceived the idea and already had a framework of what it would need.

Part of Drake's mission was to secretly put the device in Jeoung's private quarters. So, everything happening in his quarters would be transmitted to Jaqlyn's laboratory.

It was the perfect plan.

27 | JAQLYN

PREDICTABLY, JEOUNG DID EXACTLY WHAT Jaqlyn expected him to do.

Laylen brought Jaqlyn a video recording of the meeting.

Watching the recording, she heard Jeoung speak. "I have it on good authority that Jaqlyn Ilichova has formed a new lair. She has an army, and I know she is coming for me. She wants me gone so she can take my position and rule this coven. We must end her!"

The Gha'ueos listened, waiting for Jeoung to give them an order. "Just like we did many years ago with the Grimoir cult, we must end her army." The Gha'ueos made the solidarity sign—right hand, four fingers across the heart. "When I asked you to wait for the right time after we discovered that human cult, I knew what I was doing. Are we not here now? Are you not the most powerful Gha'ueos in the coven? If we had taken them out immediately when we discovered them, Jaqlyn would still be in this coven, and you would not be so powerful. Just as I knew what I was saying then, I know what I am saying now. Any questions?" he demanded.

"Where is her lair?" one shouted across the room.

"According to my source, about 1,100 kilometers from here. But we do not move until I say it is time. Do you understand?"

"Yes!" they said in unison.

"How typical!" Jaqlyn murmured when the recording finished playing. She was pleased with what she'd gathered from the short meeting—she had Jeoung right where she wanted.

It was now time to return to the coven, but she was not sure what would happen. Despite the evidence, she knew that Jeoung was also a master of deception. He would try to turn the entire situation to his benefit.

Therefore, she decided to return to the coven with a few of her best fighters. If things go south, they would fight or kill their way out of the coven and return home to their lair.

Kallista was one of the fighters she chose, simply because she was her best fighter and most valuable asset.

The old coven had changed so much in the years since she had been gone. Where she expected growth, there was only regression. Where she expected development, there was degeneration. Still, she rang the emergency bell and was escorted into the coven of Zhovs.

"How dare you show your face here again? You know there is nothing but death waiting for you here!" Jeoung shouted with glee. The way he saw it, Jaqlyn had walked into her own grave.

The other Zhovs stared at her as if she were mad. Her fighters rallied around her, ready to fight if they must.

"You see, Jeoung, I would not be back here if there was truly nothing but death waiting for me."

She turned toward the others.

"I have been gone for eighty plus years and do you see what has happened to the coven in my absence? I see vampires hiding from the sun because their sunlight bands have been damaged, and there is no one else with the skills or knowledge to repair them. I see the coven in considerable disrepair—walls falling apart, cracks in the structure, uncleanness, and windows boarded. Did you Zhovs forget that maintenance is important? We might be immortals, but the structures we built are not. Surely you have not forgotten the days before the Holmium deaths. I hear that's how you're calling that time now."

"Somebody shut her up!" Jeoung shouted.

"I have an indisputable piece of evidence about the Holmium deaths here with me," Jaqlyn said. "It shows that Jeoung knew about the Grimoir cult long before he told the Zhovs. Of course, he kept the information to himself to use it as a means to take my head off."

"That is preposterous! Surely none of you believe this banished witch!" Jeoung sounded confident, but she saw the doubt in his eyes.

"See for yourself," said Jaqlyn as she motioned for one of her men to play the recording. The video was projected on the walls directly in front of the council.

"Time to face the reaper, Jeoung," she whispered in his direction.

The Zhovs watched the confession and were in shock.

It was the worst scandal to rock the coven in a long time. Some Zhovs considered it an act of treason. It was over for Jeoung, but Jaqlyn knew he would not back down. As expected, Jeoung leaped from his high seat in the dome with a dagger in hand and headed straight for Jaqlyn, anger and mania etched on his face. Kallista was much faster and took him down before he realized what was happening.

As he regained his footing, there was hate in his eyes. "What sorcery is this?" he asked in shock as Kallista pushed him back with one hand.

"That was my experiment and the pregnancy you banished me for."

The Zhovs looked bewildered as Kallista beat one of their best fighters like it was nothing. Jeoung had gone unchallenged for so long because they considered his fighting skills unmatched. He had killed every challenger. Yet this young vampire had just outwitted him and landed him on his butt.

"You're an abomination!" Jeoung spat out as he tried to land a blow.

"And you're weak," Kallista said with disgust while deflecting his strikes. Then, in a move faster than light, she knocked Jeoung to the floor again. This time, she held him there. "Stay down like the dog you are, or I will kill you before you take your next breath."

He glared up at her with belligerence, rage, and fear. If the hatred he had in his eyes were arrows, every inch of her body would have been punctured.

Jaqlyn looked at Kallista standing over Jeoung and smiled.

"Oh, Kallista. Don't be a disappointment. Kill him. It's simple enough, isn't it?"

Cathelyna was the first to speak. "In light of this new evidence, I motion that Jaqlyn's banishment is rescinded immediately."

"Yes, yes," the council agreed.

Decisions were reversed in favor of Jaqlyn. She now had everything she wanted and had been working toward for a long time. Jaqlyn looked around the room at the faces staring back at her. Although the room was frigid, she did not focus on that. There was an air of expectancy as they waited for her to proclaim her leadership.

As Jaqlyn spoke to the council, dark clouds rolled outside, lightning struck, and thunder roared. The powerful beam from the overhead bulbs seemed to redirect the light, making her the cynosure of all eyes in attendance.

Hanging on the walls were portraits of the past members of the council, all sporting the same somber expressions of boredom and self-importance. To Jaqlyn, it felt as though their eyes were also watching her, judging her, and waiting for her proclamation.

"I will return, but I have conditions," she finally said, confidently so. She was not blind to the situation of the coven. They needed her, and she intended to take full advantage of that opportunity.

"What are they?" the council asked in unison.

"One, I take Jeoung's position. Next, my new army comes with me, and they will be assimilated into the current one based on their abilities. And last, I will continue my work in my lab."

The council members looked around at each other, each slowly nodding their heads. Then, Cathelyna looked directly at Jaqlyn and said, "Agreed."

Jaqlyn immediately made her first judgment as head of the council. She turned to Jeoung, still held down by Kallista, and said, "Jeoung, for the deaths of hundreds of vampires in the Holmium deaths, I sentence you to die." As she spoke, she smiled and nodded at Kallista with a meaningful look.

"You can't do that!" he screamed right before Kallista drove the Holmium blade she held deep into his heart. In his eyes, his look shifted from shock to pain to the realization that this was his end. He opened his mouth to say something, but the words never came.

He quickly disintegrated into a pile of ashes.

28 | KALLISTA

"IT'S RIDICULOUS THAT WE ARE giving these lowlifes relevance by keeping their cult artifacts in our coven. We must destroy everything at once!" Jaqlyn said to Drake after he told her about the room underneath the dome. It was where Jeoung had kept souvenirs gathered from the Grimoir stronghold after the vampires defeated them. "What was so important he felt the need to save it?"

"There was a portrait of the Grimoir leader along with some Holmium weapons," Drake replied.

"Why would he keep a portrait of their leader?"

"Because he was never caught. Jeoung thought it was because he escaped before we could get to him. He thought having the portrait would make it easier to find him."

"That is disturbing information. Why didn't the elite look for this man?" Jaqlyn asked.

"We searched for him for a long time, but it seems he disappeared."

"The leader had elements of magic in him. It would be impossible to forge a Holmium weapon otherwise."

Kallista had stood watch quietly as Jaqlyn talked to Drake. There was nothing for her to say, and even if there were, no one would listen.

The three of them marched down the winding stairs leading to the room in the cellar. The portrait was covered with a dark cloth. From where Kallista stood, she could see everything. The Holmium weapons were kept in a sealed lead box, but she knew what they were because she could still feel their energy.

Drake pulled the cloth away from the portrait, and Kallista noticed Jaqlyn's skin turn pasty.

As Jaqlyn looked at the picture, she crept closer to it. She was in what appeared to be a trance-like state, not blinking once. She stared at it silently for minutes, then suddenly she blinked several times as if she had just awakened. It was apparent she knew the man in the portrait.

"Burn the portrait! This man will never be found."

Drake carried out Jaqlyn's command without hesitation. However, Kallista's curiosity was piqued. She waited until they were back in the coven alone to ask Jaqlyn about the portrait.

"You know that man. Who is he?"

Jaqlyn stared at her for a moment. In that brief time, Kallista saw many emotions flash across her mother's face. "If we were to speak like humans, I would say that man was your father. But, in reality, he was part of my experiment, merely the man that donated the sperm needed to create you."

She said the words matter-of-factly, then she walked out of the castle, leaving Kallista all alone. There would be no explanation beyond what she was told. Kallista had learned to read her mother's mood. In this case, she'd no longer discuss the matter with her, so she decided to keep all her questions to herself. That man and his history would not be coming back, ever.

Based on how Jaqlyn said it, she assumed he was dead and that Jaqlyn had killed him. She harbored no resentment against her for it. It no longer mattered because she belonged nowhere.

As the days passed, Jaqlyn continued reigning over the coven. However, for Kallista, the coven felt like prison. The new coven was not home. Instead, it was an exhibition, and she was the main attraction everyone wanted to see her, Jaqlyn's creation. She was a pariah, a beautiful and skillful pariah, so they were as fascinated as they were disgusted by her.

Whenever she walked in the sun, they would always glance at her wrists, looking for a sunlight band, but she wore none. Even her immunity to Holmium was scandalous. In everyone's eyes, she was dangerous and should be avoided. Had she not effortlessly killed one of the greatest fighters they knew? Had she not driven a Holmium blade into Jeoung without effort? They hated everything about her but could do nothing about it, which made them hate her even more.

She was the creature who challenged them. She was not of pure blood, yet she was better than them.

Kallista stayed because she thought she had a family in the coven. Besides, where else would she go? Who else would understand what she was? When it turned out that the coven would never accept her, she was convinced she had no choice but to stay.

"I will prove myself to them. I will make the coven love me," she swore to herself. She trained, scouted, and volunteered for everything. But things got worse. For the other vampires, she was the hybrid vampire who would do anything asked just to prove she was better.

She bore the hate and jealousy until she could not any longer. She bore it until her eyes fully opened, and she realized she would never belong to the coven and neither would she belong to the human world. She was the first and last of her kind. She had no family, and she would stop trying to find one. She would strike out on her own and become an individual who rode solo—one without rules or boundaries. She was done being tethered down by the wills and laws of others. She would let the world take care of her. She would let nothing stop her.

Five years later, to avoid constant shame and innuendos flung at her from birth, she walked out of the coven unnoticed. She swore she would never return and took the one thing that would protect her against both man and vampire: a Holmium blade.

29 | KALLISTA

HER EYES DROPPED TO THE limp body of George on the floor, and she felt a tinge of regret that passed almost as quickly as it arrived. When she fed on him, she didn't intend to kill him, but Kallista was hungrier than she had realized.

A week passed since George's death. Kallista stood beneath an old burr oak tree in the woods behind her house and noticed the sun coming out. While out on a hunt for a rabbit or other small animal she was interrupted by a young boy with curly red hair in blue jeans and a black NASCAR T-shirt. He looked like a high school student. She tried to pacify her urge, but it had been several days since she'd had a proper feeding. The smell of his young, sweet blood reached her olfactory senses at once. The thirst overpowered her consciousness and surged to the point she attacked the young boy without warning and with such ferocity he was depleted in no time.

After regaining her senses, she gazed down at his dead body and wondered what he was doing here so many miles from the nearest town and so early in the morning. She bought her home far away from the city to ensure complete privacy.

"Who are you and what were you doing here?" she asked pointlessly.

The thought of George crossed her mind. It had been five days since she ended the relationship with George as well as his life. Clearly, it was time to find someone else.

"Where is Jackson?" she heard someone behind her ask in the distance.

"I don't know. I think he went this way," a feminine voice replied.

"This was a stupid idea. I'm never going hiking with you guys again!"

Kallista looked at the boy's neck and saw the puncture wounds had already closed. With a swish of air, she was gone.

"Did you just hear something?" the girl asked as they approached the clearing.

"I didn't—" the other boy started to say before he saw his friend's lifeless body on the ground.

Their screams resonated through the air as they rushed to Jackson's side, but it was too late. He was dead, and whoever or whatever killed him was nowhere in sight.

When Kallista arrived back home, the phone was ringing. It was rare for her to get a call. She kept a close circle and hardly ever conversed with anyone over the phone. Nevertheless, she picked up the receiver, more out of curiosity than anything else.

"Hello?" she asked.

"Hello. Am I speaking to Miss Kallista?"

"Yes. Who is this?"

"My name is Simon Wembley. I am George Hanson's lawyer."

Kallista paused for a moment. She didn't understand why George's lawyer would call her. "Yes, Mr. Wembley. How may I help you?"

"In light of Mr. Hanson's recent death, I reviewed his will and found that he left most of his assets and possessions to you."

For the first time in her life, she was in a situation that rendered her speechless.

"Are you there?"

"Sorry. Yes, yes. I am here."

"We need to meet to go over the details."

Lost in thought, she stared into the distance as the lawyer told her his address.

"Ms. Kallista, are you there?

"I have the address, I will be there." She hung up the phone.

Sometimes, she could feel her human side take over her mind. Those moments were always fleeting, as this one was bound to be as well. But here it was, a slight twinge of regret at having killed George. He had unknowingly left everything he worked hard to acquire to his killer. She sighed, and the twinge was no more.

In the distance, she heard the wailing sounds of police sirens and took a deep breath. That was the kind of disturbance she had been trying to avoid when she purchased her home. She looked around and exhaled, realizing she had nothing in her home that might pique the police's interest when they came calling. Given that her house was the closest to the dead kid, she was sure they would come knocking on her door. She could still taste the boy's blood on her tongue—the sweet aftertaste was as addictive as opium.

They would be at her door soon, asking questions and probing into her life. But she was ready for them. As if on cue, she heard a car arrive, and moments later, several quick footsteps onto her front porch. Then the doorbell rang. It was strange to listen to the ringing echo through the house. Having people standing on her porch made her irritable to the point of wanting to rip them open. But these were the police. If something happened to them, more officers would come looking. No matter how strong she was, she could not afford that complication. She had to accept the fact she couldn't just kill every person she wanted to.

"Douglas County Sheriff's Department! Anyone in?"

Kallista hid her fangs and put on a mask of a pleasant disposition before opening the door.

"Hello, officers," she said in a highly provocative voice. They stared at her for a moment, both seeming to forget for the slightest moment why they were there.

"Officers?" Kallista prompted them. Aware of the effect she had on men, she broadened her smile and turned her eyes toward them. One officer was short and much older. The other was young, tall, and slender. Both officers looked as if they were drowning in the silver depths of Kallista's eyes and could not get enough. "Officers? Is there a problem?"

The younger officer was first to return to his senses and nudged the Sheriff with his elbow to focus. The smile on her face was fixed, but underneath it all, her impatience was reaching its peak. As she stared at the two love-struck officers, she shook her head at the gullibility and predictability of humans.

"Are you going to speak or not?" she said as the impatience in her voice cut through both officers' reverie.

"Yes, ma'am. We are terribly sorry to disturb you. I'm Deputy Ajamu Manning, and this is Sheriff Loid Wilson—."

Sheriff Wilson interrupted, "We're here to ask if you've heard or seen anything unusual or suspicious in the last few hours, like someone running or maybe lost in the woods. Anything like that?"

She feigned recalling the last few hours and eventually said, "No, Sheriff. What is the problem? It's rare to have the Sheriff's department come knocking around here."

"Yes, you're right," Sheriff Wilson said. As he spoke, it was clear he was trying to project an air of authority in front of the woman. "I'm afraid someone died in the woods just off your property."

"Oh my! Are you serious?" Kallista exclaimed as she placed her hand over her heart in a dramatic move. "What happened?"

"It looks like the victim may have had a heart attack, but his friends think there was foul play," he said. "We are still waiting for the medical examiner to arrive."

"Wow! How could a young boy just die of a heart attack?"

"I don't—" Deputy Manning began to say before his eyes narrowed as Kallista's words sank into his consciousness.

"How do you know it was a boy? We never mentioned anything about a boy," he said as he reached for his gun.

Kallista folded her arms and shifted in her stance. "You mentioned his friends, so I assumed it was a male."

"Ma'am?" Sheriff Wilson said as they both drew their weapons.

Both men gasped as they watched Kallista's eyes turn from a mesmerizing silver to a violent, fiery blood-orange that sent fear into their hearts.

"What the hell?" Deputy Manning shouted even as he kept his gun aimed at her center. Kallista did not say a word. She only stared at them. Using mind control, she projected thoughts into their heads. "You both knocked on my door. I opened the door. You asked me if I saw a trespasser around my property and I said no. You think I'm a harmless lady, and you are convinced that the boy died of natural causes."

After the projection, Deputy Manning said, "Thanks again, ma'am. Have a good day." He appeared visibly baffled that his service revolver was in his hands. They excused themselves and returned to their vehicle.

"That was a close one," she mumbled to herself with a grimace. She had made a rookie mistake, one she wouldn't have made if she were in the right frame of mind. The whole George affair had left her distracted and unfocused. It was time to see George's lawyer, take possession of her newfound wealth, and close that chapter of her life completely.

30 | KALLISTA

"PLEASE, COME IN," THE LAWYER said when Kallista knocked on his door. His office had a quiet dignity about it. There were genuine mahogany leather chairs and an office table made of Elmwood inside. From all the indications, he was the lawyer that only represented the blue blood—old money. It made perfect sense he would be George's lawyer.

The office was vast and occupied the entire 16th floor west end corridor of the building. It also had two large floor-to-ceiling windows on the wall behind the desk that provided incredible views in two directions—a picturesque garden to the east and a full view of the city to the north. The two remaining walls sported floor-to-ceiling built-in bookshelves filled with lots of thick, bound books. On a wall beside one shelf was a single oil painting, *A Vase of Flowers* by Vincent van Gogh. The gleaming brown surface of his desk was uncluttered—a MacBook Pro, a leather notebook, and a framed photograph of a woman and a boy.

The lawyer was a potbellied man with a receding hairline. He had a sharp look about him that Kallista interpreted as a depth of intelligence hiding underneath his pale blue eyes. She did not need to read his mind to know what was going through it. She knew he was thinking the same thing that any sane person would in the same situation: Who are you? Why did George leave all his money to you?

"My name is Simon Wembley. And, as I explained on the phone, I am George's lawyer. I was George's lawyer, rather."

She smiled as he hung her coat on the coat tree near the door. He offered her a seat in one of the two padded Queen Anne armchairs in front of his desk. As she sat, she decided she would not tolerate unnecessary questions. Accepting George's money would come with much responsibility. She enjoyed her current routine, just the way it was. She had gifts other people would kill for:

eternal youth and beauty that made men weep. That was enough to keep her financially afloat and happy through many years on earth.

"Miss…" the lawyer started but paused when he realized there was no last name in the will.

"Just Kallista. That's my name," she said, fixing him with a steely stare.

"Well," he said as he paused with his palms flat on the desk and held her gaze for several uncomfortable seconds. "Well," he said again as he resumed his composure and the task at hand. "For the longest time, George's will stated that his properties were to be donated to charity when he passed. But a few months ago, he changed his mind and willed it all to you." Mr. Wembley looked at her, expecting a reaction, but there was none. He cleared his throat awkwardly and continued. "I hope you don't mind, but George's family has asked to meet you. They are curious about the woman who made such a significant impact on George's life that he would change his will."

Kallista stared at the lawyer and thought about his request. She did not want to meet any of George's family members and had no business with them. "Do they want to challenge the will?" she asked.

The whole situation was suspicious enough, but she suspected they may try to kick-start an investigation into George's death. If they did, she knew her only option would be to reject whatever claim the will gave her to George's properties and walk away. An autopsy had already been carried out and indicated that George had died of a heart attack. They had no basis for any lawsuit, but Kallista knew how humans thought, especially those with some level of affluence and influence. *An older man, a beautiful young woman. All she wanted was his money—it had to be foul play.*

"No, not at all. George was in his right mind when he amended his will, and he died of natural causes. There is no indication of foul play involved here. I think they are curious about who you are. It is just a simple request."

"I have the right to refuse to see them, yes?"

"Well… yes. But are you sure? They would like to meet you. And, considering all that George willed to you, it's only appropriate for you to allow them to meet the woman he was in love with and wanted to marry."

"Perhaps you're right. But I'm not interested."

The rest of the meeting went by in a blur. When it was over, Kallista was a wealthy woman. George was well off than she had imagined—he had houses all over the world, millions in liquid cash, and investments virtually everywhere.

"Congratulations again, Miss Kallista. I recommend you get a lawyer to handle your affairs. I would be remiss if I didn't let you know I'd love to be your lawyer and offer my services to you. You will not find better service elsewhere."

Kallista stared at the lawyer intently, knowing everything going through his mind. George had been one of his top clients, and now she was just as rich as he once was. He was trying to fill the profitable client void that George's account had represented.

"I'll let you know if I need your help. Thank you."

It was a surreal experience for Kallista. The little prick of compassion she felt when George died was far gone now. All she felt now was a weird sense of bewilderment mixed with elation at the fact she now had more money than she could have ever dreamed of.

However, one thing was clear to Kallista: she had no interest in managing any of George's firms or owning any of his houses. She would sell everything, and she would need help to do that.

31 | KALLISTA

KALLISTA WALKED OUT OF A trendy corner café in downtown Perry Street with a cup of coffee in her hands for appearances. She had little to do on that lazy, chilly winter day. The weather was perfect for a walk, so she window-shopped as she thought of all the things she would do with her new wealth. Upon approaching a new high-rise apartment being built at the next intersection, she did not immediately notice one woman, whose dark hair flowed, standing still and facing her direction on her side of the street. As Kallista got a few more steps closer, she realized that the woman was Jaqlyn.

She stopped. Her focus was so intense, and the moment so incredulous. Jaqlyn was the only person she saw. The background noises receded until she could hear nothing but Jaqlyn's footsteps toward her. It had been a long time since she'd seen the woman that birthed her. However, for Kallista, it could never be long enough. All she remembered was that for the longest time, she had been under the manipulating influence of this woman who now stood in front of her. It was only apt they would meet again in such frigid conditions, which correctly characterized the relationship they once shared.

Standing about four feet apart, Jaqlyn spoke first. "Hello, Kallista." Her voice had not changed, and Kallista felt silly for expecting she would sound different.

Kallista stared but said nothing. She felt nothing for her—not hate or love, just a complete absence of emotions. Sometimes she wondered how she would have turned out under different circumstances. Would she have had better regard for human life if she had been raised in a better environment? She knew of a few vampires who had gone against their first urges and had embraced the good. But she was not one of those. For her, humans were toys to manipulate, exploit, and use for her own personal gain. Evil and good were classifications that never existed when she was a child.

"What do you want?" she asked. "I should have known that little weasel Laylen would tell you where to find me." Kallista watched as fire flashed in Jaqlyn's eyes, knowing she was still the same opportunistic bitch she had always been.

They stood on the sidewalk staring into each other's eyes, remembering, not regretting, and holding their grounds.

32 | JAQLYN

"YOU MUST RETURN TO THE COVEN," Jaqlyn said without preamble. She would rather be back on her throne, governing, than be here with her brat of a spawn.

Kallista let out a contrived laugh as if Jaqlyn had just made some joke. "You don't expect me to come back. You can't be that naïve."

The tone in Jaqlyn's voice matched the scorn in Kallista's eyes. She raised one side of her mouth as her silver eyes turned cold with absolute disdain. "You will do as I command! Do you understand?"

"Oh, I understand just fine," Kallista smirked as she walked up to Jaqlyn and stood toe-to-toe with her. "I understand that you forget yourself. You forget that you have no right over my actions or me. You forget that I am one of the strongest creatures on earth. You forget there is no way in hell I will go back to that graveyard you call a coven. You only want to control me, fight your battles, but worst of all, you want to experiment on me. I am nothing to you but a lab specimen. You were never a mother, never wanted to be a mother, and will never be a mother to me."

Jaqlyn was good at hiding her emotions, but she could not conceal how furious her spawn's words had made her. Never had anyone refused her, knowing the cost of their disobedience would have been their lives. But she needed Kallista, which gave the spoiled brat the upper hand. Besides, she wasn't sure she could beat Kallista in a physical battle if it came to it. "You will do as I command, child," Jaqlyn persisted in a harsh tone, which was more a show to appear in charge than any real expectation of authority over Kallista.

33 | KALLISTA

IN A SNAP, KALLISTA PUSHED Jaqlyn back against the wall, catching the older woman off guard. She did not care who was watching. All she cared about was not allowing this tyrant to rule her life ever again. She would not allow Jaqlyn to leave, thinking she still had any hold over her.

When Kallista spoke, it was through clenched teeth. "Listen to me. I am no child, Jaqlyn. No child of yours. You have forgotten yourself and need to remember who you are addressing. I am no longer one of your followers who trails behind you blindly. I am a powerful hybrid vampire you created, but I will not hesitate to kill you if you ever come back here again."

"You don't understand, Kallista. I need you back at the coven to experiment with your strengths and other powers," Jaqlyn pleaded. "I need to create more like you, stronger vampires, to grow our numbers and ensure our future. I never told you this, but you were forbidden."

"I have no interest or desire to live amongst the coven. I have my own life now, and I refuse to be any part of your experiments." After a momentary pause, she asked, "What do you mean I was forbidden?"

"If it weren't for me going against the coven's laws, against Jeoung's prohibition to create you, there would not be a Kallista. My dear, you would not be here, and I never would have been banished."

"You've told this to me before, but it appears you left parts out. All the same, it changes nothing. I don't care about you, your coven, your experiments, how I came about, or why you were banished. I owe you nothing! You say these things only to manipulate me."

Jaqlyn's eyes glowed fiery amber red with anger and humiliation. She bared her fangs in preparation to devour and destroy.

"I dare you," Kallista said as she quickly repositioned her hand to the base of her mother's throat and held her against the wall.

Some people had stopped to watch the commotion. Jaqlyn, to save face, cleared her throat and looked around at the increasing number of humans gawking before looking back at Kallista. "You are lucky we are amid these humans. You are so fortunate."

"Or you would have done what? The student has become the master. It's time to accept it. Now leave this place and never return."

Kallista released Jaqlyn and stepped back as Jaqlyn straightened up. With her eyes still locked on Jaqlyn, she said, "If I see you again, I will kill you where you stand." Then, she gave a mocking bow, turned, and walked away.

34 | LAYLEN

"WERE YOU ABLE TO CONVINCE her to return?" Laylen asked as soon as Jaqlyn walked into the dome later that evening. The sun was setting, burning a bright orange and casting an ambient tinge over the coven. The Gha'ueos stood in corners of the room as her anger pulsated. Laylen asked before noting the atmosphere, and the last word he spoke was drawn out as he came to that realization.

"Convince her? Is the situation so precarious?" Jaqlyn's voice thundered. Her fangs protruded from the corners of her mouth, and her eyes glowed in their sockets. She raced from her seat to where Laylen stood and pinned him to the wall before he could blink. His fear saturated him like water on a drowning rat. "You disgust me!" she snarled, flinging him away like a dirty rag.

Laylen scrambled to his feet and tried to gather his composure. Even though it appeared he may lose his life, he then realized something good had come out of the visit—Jaqlyn now understood how difficult her daughter was to persuade.

"Jaqlyn, I promise you I shall think of something. Kallista will come home," Laylen said before scurrying out of the room and leaving Jaqlyn lost in thought.

Later that night, Laylen stood outside the dome and looked up into the sky. The sun had gone to rest and the moon, providing a much-needed guide and calm, had taken its place. The moon. He was now ready to approach Jaqlyn to tell her his new plan—even though none of the previous ones had worked, and there was no guarantee the new one would work either. He slowly closed his eyes, regained his confidence, and let his worries dissipate like smoke floating up through an endless night.

He pushed open one of the tall double doors leading into the dome and peered inside. The first thing that struck him was that the Gha'ueos were not there. Being in that sacred space with only Jaqlyn was strange. She was powerful now, and even though she had not reached the age to be titled an elder, they all knew she essentially was one. Times had changed for them all, and it was time the coven claimed an elder. Laylen felt Jaqlyn would be the first choice. She was not an elder and neither were any of the other council members, but she was the eldest.

With her plan to birth purebloods, she could be well on her way to creating a new era for the vampires—the age of Distinction. The thought left a good taste in his mouth. Jaqlyn would make a great leader on their way to global domination. He could picture the future when vampires would not have to hide. They would hold the world's powers in their hands, and there would be peace in the world once the humans had a central authority to report to.

Jaqlyn had the same cold expression she had every time she saw him, but now there was something different about it—a bit of warmth. He was grateful and willing to do anything to get that warmth to increase.

"Laylen, do you have a plan, or do you want me to replace you with someone else?"

He knew what she meant. If he made the mistake of not delivering on this task, he was done. There was no way he would get back into her good graces again. This task was a test, and it was one he had to ace. He believed his new plan would work if Jaqlyn gave him the go-ahead.

"I have a strategy in place, and I am confident it will work this time."

"Tell me what you have in mind," she said.

"Kallista is a strong-willed woman. She does not want to see you, she will not return on her own free will, and I do not believe we would be able to abduct her."

Jaqlyn laughed aloud. "You? Abduct Kallista? Is that a joke?"

"No, I do not intend to," Laylen said, knowing Kallista was stronger than the other vampires, and given the hard training she received from Jaqlyn herself, there was no way she could be abducted using force. On top of that, he was susceptible to Holmium.

"So, what is your plan?"

"I need your permission to follow her for a while. That way, I can become familiar with her routine and discover her weakness."

"Weakness? I trained her to have no weaknesses. You won't find any." Jaqlyn looked insulted by the idea.

"I mean no disrespect, but you have not lived with Kallista for over a hundred years. She has obviously changed and may have developed some habits we can't explain."

Rubbing her chin, Jaqlyn said, "You might be right. Can you assure me that this plan of yours will work?"

"Yes, what I intend to do is—"

Jaqlyn raised a hand up, cutting him off. "I don't care about the details. You have a limited amount of time to make sure it comes to fruition. If you do not have positive results by the time my patience expires, I will replace you with another who is more than eager to take your place and can get the job done."

Laylen knew he had no reason to speak any other words. The meeting was over. It was now time to get out of the dome and put his plan into action. He would need a few other vampires to accomplish his mission, which Jaqlyn would approve.

He was not the commander of the army, but as Jaqlyn's apprentice and inner circle, the other vampires respected him. The coven had progressed immensely since Jaqlyn's return. There were modern buildings constructed all over the place, but the one that struck him the most was the lab. In place of her old laboratory, the same building where she had created Kallista, there was a new laboratory filled with ultramodern equipment. It was the first building Jaqlyn rebuilt when she seized power. While Jeoung had been content with sitting on the highest chair in the dome, Jaqlyn wanted more. She wanted vampires to feel they were at the top of the food chain and were superior to humans in every way. Being surrounded by modern buildings and the most advanced technology available was part of achieving this goal.

Laylen walked into the training room and saw the commander—tall and intimidating with permanently narrowed eyes. He was instructing the new Gha'ueos in advanced combat techniques. The training was very intense, and sometimes careless vampires lost their lives learning how to defend against Holmium-forged weapons. Despite the occasional loss, Jaqlyn's army was getting better and growing stronger. When it came to instruct the new vampire recruits, Drake was the best.

Just another good officer whose potential was being wasted until Jaqlyn relieved the old commander of his position and declared it open. The days of assuming positions based on a vampire's closeness to Jeoung were over. The Gha'ueos had to compete for the available spot. They were judged by the Zhovs under Jaqlyn's watchful eyes, and the results were outstanding. Drake had ultimately proven he was the right person to command her army. The stability and progress Jaqlyn had introduced into the coven made the vampires bow to her leadership. It was her time now, and Laylen knew she would hold that position for a long, long time.

"Drake!" he called. The commander raised a hand, signaling a pause in the training. He turned around, and Laylen recognized his expression—brazen displeasure. Everyone knew how much Drake hated being interrupted during training exercises.

But when he saw the person who had interrupted him, his expression eased a little. "Laylen!" he said with open arms. "To what do I owe this pleasure?"

"Drake. Good to see you, brother."

"What can I do for you?"

Putting a hand on Drake's back in a move that showed the men were close, Laylen led him outside of earshot. "I need two soldiers for a covert mission for

Jaqlyn. They should be well-trained in stealth and combat."

"Of course. I have two I can recommend."

That was all it took. Two seasoned soldiers were Laylen's to command. Drake assured him Taylor and Demetri could be trusted and their discretion was guaranteed.

"The plan is simple," he instructed the two soldiers. "You will take turns watching Kallista and report everything she does to me. If you get caught, there will be hell to pay."

He watched their eyes grow wider as they stared at him, aghast.

"*The* Kallista?" the taller one asked.

"Yes, *the* Kallista," Laylen reassured. "Jaqlyn wants to bring her home, and our job is to observe her routine and see if there is a way we can lure her back. Be on the lookout for something that may make her want to return. Do you understand?"

"Yes…"

It looked like they had something else to say. "Yes? What is it?"

"I have heard she is immune to Holmium. Is this true?"

"Yes, which is why you have to be extremely careful not to be seen."

"Yes, sir!" They snapped to attention with eyes forward.

The instructions were acknowledged and understood. It was time to put Laylen's plan into motion.

35 | KALLISTA

A BOTTLE OF CHATEAU MARGAUX 2009 Balthazar lay open at Kallista's feet as she curled up beside her window. The only thing red wine had going for it was its resemblance to blood. The tangy, slightly bitter taste was not bad either. It was one drink she could honestly say she enjoyed.

She settled on her couch and looked out at the moon. The stars in the night sky fascinated her. Ever-enduring, shining in the cloudless night, accentuated by the inky darkness of the sky. It felt a little like the same darkness within her soul. Sometimes she wanted it gone and wished she could have been a better person. But it was too late for her. Her die had been cast a long time ago.

A sudden restlessness interrupted her thoughts. Before she knew it, it had suffused her entire system and left her on edge. She had to do something to ease it—she had to feed.

Abruptly, Kallista stood and walked into her closet. She would need something light and comfortable to hunt. After a moment, she found the perfect outfit. It was mostly made of latex and felt like a second skin, hugging her breasts, and causing them to jut out and look pronounced. The curve of her waist broadened into a noticeable flare of her hips.

As she prepared, her anticipation grew until she felt ravenous. Her prey tonight would be unfortunate. Her hunger combined with the residual anger from the encounter with Jaqlyn made an explosive combination.

Kallista walked down the sidewalk and scouted.

When he came along, she displayed a predator's smile. He was perfect prey—he reeked of hopelessness and alcohol. When she listened to his thoughts, they were the most revealing she had heard all night. He'd had a rough day—a rough life, for that matter—and was considering suicide. His daughter had died in a fire, his wife had recently left him, and he had lost his job. He had hit rock bottom, and as much as he tried, he just couldn't see tendencies of anything good happening.

Kallista would be doing him a favor by ridding him of his pain. She ducked into the shadows as he staggered past her. Behind him, Kallista darted from cover to cover, remaining motionless each time he glanced back. His fear heightened. The combination of blood, alcohol, and fear ignited bloodlust in Kallista. His blood called to her, her fangs were ready. She laughed wickedly, sending a chilling sound that echoed around the empty streets.

"Who's there? Show yourself!" he called out.

Kallista could wait no longer. She suddenly swooped on him and had him pinned to the ground in no time at all.

"What are you?" were the last words he spoke. She grinned at him evilly just a second before sinking her fangs into his neck.

His blood was perfect, tinged with alcohol and spiced with fear. It was the most fulfilling feed in a long time. The pleasures felt demanded to be expressed and screamed into the night. Her eyes were blazing blood-orange, hair flaming amber-red, and she could feel the blood traveling through her entire body. Her cells had awakened and she felt alive. This was the real definition of freedom and beauty.

Her skin came alive, the paleness disappearing from every inch of her body. It was the most remarkable thing, an irony of life she would not attempt to unravel.

She felt his body quiver then went limp in her hands, but she did not stop drinking. She drank her fill and then drank more until his skin took on a pallor that was devoid of life. Kallista continued feeding and at that moment, what she wanted was the only thing that mattered.

If she wanted something, she would take. It was the way of the world—the forceful taking from the weak, predators consuming preys. Her humanity was the only thing stopping her from painting the town red with human blood and leaving a trail of bodies in her wake.

She pushed herself off the man and stood over his body. He was only a vessel now. She had freed his soul to a place devoid of pain. He would be happier for it. She had tasted the misery in his blood and had seen his memories as the blood flowed down her throat. She had done him a favor—at least that was what she told herself.

"Rest easy, fella," she whispered softly as she walked away, feeling livelier. The puncture wounds were already gone as soon as she licked them. It would be another heart attack for local law enforcement. No evidence, no witnesses, no suspects.

Now that she had fed, she had other things to tend to. The restlessness that plagued her was gone entirely, so she could focus on the next issue of importance—selling off George's assets. And she knew just the man to call.

In the distance not too far behind her, two vampires watched as she walked away from the body. There was something about Kallista that left them in awe. Perhaps it was her beauty, or it may have been the finesse with which she had hunted. Whatever it was, it was something worth admiring.

The Gha'ueos they called Taylor, short and stocky, was so caught up in watching Kallista that he accidentally kicked an empty paint can. It hit a brick wall. The resulting noise was as loud as a shotgun in the desert—it echoed out into the empty night, and both vampires became motionless, fearing the worst.

But whatever thoughts occupying Kallista's mind had saturated it entirely to the point that she didn't seem to hear anything else.

Taylor and Demetri waited under cover of darkness until she was gone.

"What the hell?" Demetri whispered loudly once she was out of earshot.

"I'm sorry. I didn't even notice that can," Taylor said, contrite.

"God damn it! Don't ever make a rookie mistake like that ever again or we're dead."

"I was just distracted. Did you see her? Damn! She's stunning!"

"And lethal, in case you forgot that!"

"Yeah, yeah. Chill out, man. It won't happen again."

"It better not. Next time, we might not live to tell the tale."

They were caught between the devil and the blue sea—it was either they pleased Laylen by successfully completing the mission or faced his wrath, or they were discovered by Kallista and faced her wrath. Either way, they were on shaky ground and could not afford any more mistakes.

36 | KALLISTA

"HELLO, WEMBLEY LAW OFFICE," ANSWERED THE RECEPTIONIST.

"Mr. Wembley, please. This is Kallista."

"Sure, Ms. Kallista. One moment please."

"Oh, Miss Kallista. It's a pleasure to hear from you. Have you decided what your next course of action will be?"

"Yes, Mr. Wembley. I want to sell off everything George willed to me. And I would like to do so as soon as possible."

For a minute, there was complete silence on the other end. It was as if the lawyer was trying to gather his thoughts. His voice, when he spoke again, was peppered with a mild shock. "Really? Everything?"

"Yes, everything. You will receive your customary percentage for every asset you sell. I need you to start making inquiries with potential buyers."

"Okay, Miss Kallista. I will do that. But first, we should meet in my office to discuss the details. What time is fine by you?"

"As early as possible. How does 8 a.m. tomorrow sound?"

"Perfect. Goodni—"

She ended the call before he could finish.

When dawn broke the next morning, Kallista was already awake. The aura of contentment she felt from the previous night was almost gone. In its place was the same increasing restlessness that prompted her to go hunting the night prior. She knew it was not bloodlust but anxiety from the need for a new man. She wanted to feel her blood grow hot from the euphoria of seduction. More than anything, she craved a man's cum gushing down her throat while listening to his groans of pleasure as her mouth encased his hot hardness. Clearly, she needed a new mark.

Kallista had always been comfortable sleeping without the restraints of clothes. For her, there was nothing as cozy as feeling the softness of her silk sheets rubbing against her skin. So, sleeping in the nude had become a regular habit. As Kallista pulled on her robe, she moved toward the window facing east and watched the sunrise over the horizon. Sometimes she genuinely appreciated the wonder of nature, including that big beautiful orange orb in the distance.

As the sun rose, despite the many things she hated about Jaqlyn, Kallista couldn't help but admit that the woman who was supposed to be her mother was an icon in the vampire world. Her talent was unrivaled by any other vampire sorceress or sorcerer, a testament to the depth of her knowledge—or perhaps her thirst for knowledge. She was a vital part of the vampire community, there was no denying it. If not for Jaqlyn, vampires would still have to hide away from the sun and stuck to hiding in the shadows of darkness.

After returning from her mental reverie, Kallista left the window and headed straight to the bathroom. She took a hot bath, dressed, and got ready to make her way to the lawyer's office. For this meeting, she was trying her best to look the part of a wealthy woman. And rightfully so.

She chose her clothes carefully, wanting to convey the image of a businesswoman who was astute and with no time for trivial matters, but one who was also relatively warm and approachable. Her dress was teal green with just enough peeking of skin, a V-neck, and a sheer waistline that accentuated her figure perfectly. She wore gold and black shoes with ankle straps. She chose the outfit that relayed the intended message perfectly well: the look of sophisticated sexuality. After applying a dash of pink lipstick and a few brushes of mascara that made her eyelashes voluminous, she was all set.

She grabbed her car keys, walked to her car, and slid into her silver-on-red Aston Martin DB11 that George had purchased for her. It would be a long and eventful day, but somehow, this was OK today.

37 | LAYLEN

IN THE DISTANCE, THE THREE Of Them Watched Kallista's. As soon as she got on the road, Taylor and Demetri followed her, but Laylen stayed back. It was time to investigate what her living space looked like. Perhaps it would provide a few insights on how he could get her back to the coven.

The house itself was an exceptional piece of real estate. Laylen could tell Kallista had chosen the house carefully—it was on a private road, and there were no neighbors for miles on either side, perfect for someone who had no interest in socializing. Getting into the house was simple for Laylen. The lock was easy to pick, and he did it in such a way she would not know anyone had been there.

Inside was clean, without a speck of dust to be seen anywhere. He assumed she must have a regular housekeeper because housecleaning did not fit Kallista's profile.

"Where do you keep it?" he asked aloud as he walked through the house. Besides finding a way to get her to return to the coven, he needed to find out if she always kept the Holmium blade on her person. Laylen walked from room to room, careful not to touch anything with his bare hands, but he found nothing of interest. The kitchen was sparkling clean, but all the cabinets were empty. The house was tastefully furnished, and he even found a few antiques scattered around. But as far as he could tell, Kallista had no apparent source of income. This gave him pause.

How, then, is she able to afford this house, her luxurious lifestyle? Where does her money come from?

The thoughts had not escaped his mind when he walked into her bedroom. When he opened the doors to the armoire, he saw the safe. The Holmium weapon was in there. He could feel the essence of the blade. As a sorcerer, Laylen had advantages only a few vampires in the world had—one was that he could tell when he was close to a Holmium-forged weapon. It had something to do with the sixth sense sorcerers must develop if they were to ever amount to anything in magic. He had honed his sixth sense over the years.

As Laylen stood in front of the safe, he knew this weapon was more dangerous than the others. Where the other Holmium weapons only had a fraction of the mineral in them, this one was made from pure Holmium. It was held together by potent magic.

When he walked out of her house after carefully returning everything to its original state, Laylen smiled. He had made a monumental discovery—Kallista did not always carry her weapon with her. Now all they had to do was get to her when she was away from home. It would be challenging but not impossible.

38 | SEBASTIÁN

SEBASTIÁN RODRIGUEZ RECEIVED THE CALL early that morning from one of his father's oldest friends, Simon Wembley. A woman who had recently come into a lot of money and assets was looking to sell the businesses and properties she had acquired. The most exciting part was that she wanted the properties sold off soon, and because of that, she would pay the real estate agent a high commission.

"The story is a peculiar one. Did you hear of George Hanson's death?"

Sebastián had to think hard but soon remembered the news reports. What was interesting was that even though he was a fit, healthy man in his fifties, he had died of a heart attack. It seemed weird to him at the time and a stark reminder of how precarious life can be.

"Yes, I did. What does Mr. Hanson have to do with this?"

"Well, the properties to be sold were all his."

"I didn't know Mr. Hanson was married."

"That's the thing, he wasn't. The woman to whom he willed his entire estate was his girlfriend."

"You've got to be kidding!" Sebastián exclaimed. It was difficult for him to understand why a man would will his entire estate to a woman who was not even his wife. He could not wait to meet the woman. Perhaps seeing her would provide some insight.

"I'm not kidding. His family doesn't seem to care very much about the estate, either."

"He was from a rich British family, was he not?"

"Yes, he was. Anyway, can you be in my office by 8 a.m. today?" Simon asked from the other end of the line.

Sebastián glanced at the clock. It was 6:10 a.m.

"Sure, I'll be there."

"Good. I want the lady to meet you so we can iron out the details of this transaction."

"Thank you for thinking of me, Simon," Sebastián said before the call ended. Time was short, so he needed to get ready for this meeting. He perceived it would be a game-changer for him.

He decided to wear his *big deal* outfit—a sharp Brooks Brothers dark blue Windowpane 2-button suit. It fit him to the T and left him looking and feeling extremely good, over-optimistic. Sebastián also had his own charm, and if the potential client was a lady, there was no harm in using his appeal to influence the chance she'd call him for any future business. Besides, it would go a long way in convincing the woman he was the right person for this job.

He arrived at Wembley & Harrison, LLC in record time. Being a former paralegal at the law firm, Sebastián surmised that whoever this client was, she must be valuable to be handled personally by the big man himself.

"Good morning, Rose," he greeted Simon's secretary.

"Sebastián!" she exclaimed as she stood and gave him a huge smile. "It's been a while."

"Yes, it has," he said with his signature grin. Rose blushed prettily at that. He still had it in him. The lady client stood no chance against his charm. "Is Simon in?"

"Yes," she said as he headed toward Simon's office. Rose caught him after a few steps and said, "He asked that you meet him in the conference room instead."

"Conference room, huh?" Sebastián raised his eyebrows. This client had to be important for Simon to meet in the conference room. That space was usually reserved for big firms with retainers of nothing less than six figures.

"Yes, maybe you'll understand better when you see the client," Rose said with a wink.

Sebastián walked into the conference room to see that Simon was already seated. It was unusual to see him waiting for a client. He was *the* Simon Wembley after all, a well-known and well-respected lawyer widely sought after and who often handled several substantial cases at a time. His clients were supposed to do the waiting.

Sebastián's wristwatch showed the time was 7:55 a.m.

"Good morning, Simon. As always, it's good to see you. And thank you again for contacting me."

"You're welcome. How is your dad? I've not spoken with him in a long while. Work has been hectic," he said, smiling.

"Yeah, I know how it is. Dad's just fine, thanks for asking," Sebastián replied and returned the smile. "You using the conference room is quite rare for a meeting. This client must be extraordinary. And you're here early too!"

Simon laughed. "The estate my client recently came into is worth about half a billion dollars."

"What?" Sebastián's smile faded.

"Yes. George Hanson was a successful businessman with an instinct for growing his business and managing a diverse portfolio. The wealth he had amassed as of his passing was a testament to his keen business acumen. Kallista, that's the client's name, has asked me to direct and oversee the complete liquidation of the estate as soon as possible."

"Wow! Wow!" Sebastián ran a hand through his hair as the information sunk in.

He had asked Simon to tell him more about her just before he heard a new set of footsteps enter the office. A strange hush fell over the office where only moments before there had been somewhat of a noticeable buzz. Now, only silence. Seated with his back angled toward the door, Sebastián did not see her enter the conference room. However, Simon did, and he hastily pushed his seat back as he got to his feet.

"Miss Kallista," he said after awkwardly clearing his throat.

"Hello, Mr. Wembley," she said.

The voice made Sebastián stand and turn around. He understood what everyone's fuss had been about as soon as he saw Kallista. He half expected her to disappear once he blinked his eyes. She was so alluring that the entire experience felt surreal. He could only stare at her.

The dress she wore was stunning and amplified her glorious silver eyes. Sebastián could almost swear it was possible to drown in those eyes. Suddenly, he felt inadequate and inferior. It was as if his expensive designer suit was now ordinary and he was nothing like a man in which she would be interested.

Why does that even matter? He asked himself.

But deep down, he knew the answer. It mattered because after seeing Kallista, he desperately wanted to catch her interest. He wanted it with such an incomprehensible intensity that he was startled at its revelation.

"Miss Kallista, please," Simon said as he hastily drew out a chair for her.

It looked to Sebastián like she was floating due to the grace with which she moved. She walked the way he imagined Cinderella would have walked in her glass slippers if the fairy tale were real. Nevertheless, *she* was real, and she was right in front of him. He could not take his eyes off her even though it was neither professional nor polite.

"Sebastián?" he dimly heard Simon say. "Sebastián?"

Hearing his name dragged his attention away from her.

"Yes?" he asked as he slowly turned his head and met Simon's eyes.

"This is Miss Kallista."

Sebastián quickly turned his attention back to Kallista.

"Miss Kallista meet Sebastián Rodriguez. He is a real estate agent, the best in the game. And, to be frank, I think he is the most capable agent around to quickly liquidate the properties."

39 | KALLISTA

KALLISTA GLANCED AT THE MAN a moment then flashed him a brilliant grin as she watched his pupils dilate in response. Her interest was piqued, studying this attractive man in his late thirties with an air of arrogance.

How predictable.

Several thoughts ran through her mind, but the chief of them was that she no longer had to find a man. The one sitting directly opposite her would do fine. He had the looks, tan complexion, sharp brown eyes, wavy black hair, and a tall, slender body. He was perfect for her purposes. She would enjoy using him to her advantage and was positive he would enjoy being used as well.

The rest of the meeting went slow. Kallista paid attention to the figures and listened as Simon Wembley gave her the details of the proposed properties for sale.

"Are you sure you want to sell the penthouse as well? It's a prime piece of real estate you should keep. The location would at least make a good vacation spot," Sebastián said.

"I'm selling everything."

She had no interest in owning property other than the place she called home. She had to move freely whenever she wished. She had moved to Castle Rock only a few years ago, but before that, she had lived in several cities. When one does not age, human admiration has a way of turning into suspicions. Kallista remembered the last time she had spent too much time in one place and what happened as a result.

It was 1966, and she had been living in Fresno, California, for fifteen years. It was a growing city at the time. She had some acquaintances—people she met through men she dated, but she gained new neighbors as subdivisions sprang up around her property. A primary reason she had purchased that place was that it was far from the city center. She also appreciated its closeness to the beautiful Millerton Lake. However, as time passed, other people from the downtown district decided they also wanted to have a house by the lake, and she had more neighbors than she could have ever imagined. It was dreadful, but she tried to make it work by limiting the frequency of her interactions with the neighbors and keeping to herself as much as she could.

Nevertheless, as much as she tried, she could not escape the notice of the husbands and the men in the neighborhood. Of course, the women's jealousy reared its ugly head at all the attention Kallista received. She had no interest in the men, but the neighborhood women were threatened anyway. Soon, rumors surfaced, and within a short period, things were out of control.

"Kallista is not normal."

"Some days, she's paler than an albino, and if you see her a few hours later, she's back to a regular complexion."

"I think she's a witch."

"She doesn't age."

"She's a devil worshiper."

She could feel a storm brewing, but she didn't think anything would come of it. Then, late one night, she woke up to a racket outside her house. When she peeked out the window, she saw a mob of mostly women who held sticks and tiki torches. Their envy and hate had turned to fear, and fear had morphed into something even more dangerous. They wanted her gone, but even more so, they wanted a pound of her flesh for their troubles, too.

She remembered ripping through them after one of them made the mistake of throwing a stick at her. She remembered the unguarded anger that overtook her. The bloodlust that made them scream with horror when she ripped the first woman's throat out. All who came to her home that night had died. Once it was over, and her eyes had cleared, she knew she could no longer live in Fresno. She left that night and never looked back.

She remembered each detail.

"Selling Everything. Right," Sebastián said with a nod.

After arrangements for the sale were in place and their business was concluded, they walked out of the office together. As Sebastián escorted her to her car, he asked, "Kallista? May I call you Kallista?"

"Yes, of course. That's my name."

"I rarely mix business with pleasure, but I'll call you in a few days so we can set a date to get to know each other better," he said, feeling sure of himself.

Kallista stopped walking, turned to him, and smiled with a devilish gleam in her eyes at his certainty.

"Sure. You do that." She was up for the challenge.

Sebastián Rodríguez's fate was sealed.

40 | SEBASTIÁN

AFTER MANY LATE NIGHTS OUT, fine dining and spending time together, they stood holding each other in his master bedroom. Even though the months had passed by quickly, the view through the glass doors overlooking the mountains was still breathtaking. His bedroom was decorated in a masculine style with stone walls with dimmable light sconces and a titanium-colored, floating king-sized bed with Lucrezia by Anichini linens and a mink coverlet.

Next to the bed was a black Hans J. Wegner Ox chair. Sebastián walked to it and took a seat, both hands gripping his kneecaps in anticipation. He then watched with pleasure as the beautiful woman in black turned to stand directly in front of him. To him, she was a work of art. He was nothing if not an aficionado of fine art.

As he watched lustfully, she playfully allowed her hands to travel over her stomach and upward until they wrapped provocatively around her breasts. Her shimmering silver eyes seemed to light up with an inner fire from being turned on, and that made him rock hard.

You love touching yourself, don't you? He thought.

He continued to stare at her with a single-minded intensity. Her generous breasts swelled over the scandalously low neckline of her dress, and Sebastián sighed with pleasure as he noticed her firm nipples pressing against the fabric.

He still did not understand why she had chosen him. Out of all the men in the world, this mysterious and wantonly beautiful woman wanted *him*. But here she was, approaching him with fire in her eyes, making him harder than he'd ever been. What he felt was beyond the physical. Something about her made him want to protect her, wrap his arms around her, and promise her everything would be all right. He wanted to be the family she didn't have and to deliver all of her wishes.

Fuck! I'm falling for her!

The realization left him stunned and a little scared. There were things about her he did not understand.

Kallista had enticed and teased him ever since the first time he set eyes on her.

Now that he knew her better, he would give everything to convince her to be his. It all seemed like a dream, something that would most likely not pass into reality. But here they were, about to share their passion for one another. What he wanted more than anything else was to have her ultimately, to bury himself to the hilt in her depths, uninhibited. However, for now, he would be satisfied with her brand of pleasure. It was unfathomable this woman was still a virgin, but he believed her when she told him. To him, she could not lie, not with the truth radiating through her luminous eyes like that. She proposed giving him oral pleasure only, and from that beautiful mouth of hers, he had no doubt it would be a heavenly experience.

He thought about how long it had taken to get to this stage with her. She had allowed him to steal a few kisses and some intimate caresses during their after-dinner stroll by the sea the times they met. Those were beautiful moments. The kissing and caressing were short but passionate enough to leave him aroused and panting like a teenage boy. To his surprise, early this morning she sent him a text message saying she would come by his house that night. The thought of her image had hijacked his attention the entire day.

Now, Sebastián gazed at the woman as he fumbled with the zipper to his pants. It was just his luck that tonight, of all nights, his zipper got temporarily caught in the fabric of his trousers in his careless and hasty eagerness to release his throbbing cock. He felt blessed that Kallista had chosen him in what was promising to be the most decadent rendezvous of his life. He had no doubt many men would kill to be in his position, and he had no intention of taking that fact for granted. Before they saw each other, he had been celibate for almost three months after a bad breakup with his cheating ex-girlfriend. The sexual drought that ensued had made for an unhappy and wary time. Thank God the drought was ending tonight. He could hardly wait to get his hands, lips, and everything else on Kallista.

He now understood in that moment of absolute clarity that George Hanson was not a fool for leaving all he had to this woman. He was merely a man in love with the most beautiful woman in the world.

Sebastián sat and watched hungrily as Kallista swayed around the room. He half hoped she would ease her gown off her shoulders and down until her nipples popped out over the edge of her dress. His mouth watered thinking about tasting those firm mounds and licking them until she begged him to take her.

She smiled at him and shook her head. It was a little unnerving, almost as though she could hear his thoughts. She had an alluring scent about her that always did something strange to him. Tonight, mixed with the expectation of coitus, the aroma got his juices flowing even more. He was now a compromised man.

He would do anything for her, she only had to ask. His biggest wish, by far, was for her to ask him to make love to her. Before tonight, every time their date ended, she would leave him with an aching heart and a stiff hard cock. Many times, he had to seek relief with his own hands. He couldn't count the number of times he had asked her to spend the night at his place. But her answer was always the same, leaving him to spend all those nights alone. This night, however, most of his lustful fantasies would finally become a reality.

As he continued to watch, her dress fell to the floor with a quiet hush. She stood before him, unabashedly naked. Sebastián was excited she had worn nothing beneath her dress. No panties. No bra. Nothing. Maybe, just maybe, she would give herself to him completely.

His desire to make love to her became mercilessly overwhelming. But he had made her a promise, and he would not break the trust she had placed in him. Perhaps she had changed her mind and was not going to let him know until the last minute. This could become the best night of his life.

"Do you like what you see?" she asked with a husky note in her voice. Lifting one delicate index finger to her mouth, she sucked it gently, giving Sebastián a tantalizing preview of what it would look like to have his cock being toyed erotically between her luscious lips. She took her wet finger and rubbed it across her left nipple until it gleamed. Then, she closed her eyes and cupped her breasts and pinched her nipples with both hands. She twisted and tweaked the left one and then the right, rolling them between her fingers with a look on her face that said she was as turned on as he was.

Sebastián had gotten so carried away by Kallista's show he had forgotten he had yet to get his pants off. As he continued to watch her fondle her own nipples, he attacked his fly again with a near-desperate effort. With a groan of relief, he finally shoved his pants down enough to pull out his engorged cock. He watched as her smile widened. She loved what she saw, and it pleased him to no end. It was a massive stroke to his ego.

Slowly, she approached him and enclosed his cock in a firm grip. His eyes closed for a moment as he soaked in the pleasure of her soft palm, touching him. She began to lightly stroke his shaft, and his eyes snapped wide open to stare at her hand, teasing his hardened flesh.

As she continued to handily deliver him some long overdue pleasure, the moment he almost came undone was when he looked into her eyes—there was a fire in her eyes, he could not explain. She stared at his cock as if she wanted to devour it. His passion was so intense, he could imagine making love to her until she was virtually catatonic.

She stared at him as she removed her hand from his shaft, then she licked her lips. Instead of wrapping her mouth around him as he was expecting, she shifted away, looked back, and smiled at him. Her silver eyes looked sultry, and he shook his head out of pity for himself. He could no longer deny the obvious. He belonged to her now, mind, body, and soul.

When Kallista turned back around, she was only a few feet away. Again, she trailed her fingers across the gentle curve of her stomach, stopping for a moment to touch her navel. When he realized what she was contemplating, his eyes popped wide open as he followed the direction of her hands.

"Damn!" he muttered.

Everything she was doing was so provocative he could not help but touch himself while he watched. He wrapped a hand around his cock and stroked himself as her hands moved lower and traced the shaved skin around her vagina. She eased onto bent knees, then sat on the rug, leaned her body backward, spread her legs wide, and parted her lips with both hands to show him the beautiful pink folds which had become the center of his universe. As one finger slid over the small nub of her clitoris, her back arched into the movement. He watched, hypnotized, as she masturbated by sticking her middle finger deep in and out of her hot channel.

God, I want to fuck you!

Sebastián couldn't tear his eyes away from her, and he couldn't stop fondling himself in response. She withdrew her finger and held it out so he could see it glistening from her wetness. Then, she brought her hand up and spread those luscious juices onto her firm nipples, causing them to shine.

"Well? Do you like what you see?" she asked in her singsong voice. The way she spoke had always intrigued him. Her tone, the movement of her lips, everything about her fascinated him to no end. That question, uttered in a sultry voice, drew his gaze back up to meet hers. He nodded and licked his lips again. "Would you like to taste my nipples?"

He felt uneasy, nervous in his stomach. He could not believe how far Kallista would go to turn him on, not after she had told him explicitly there would be no sex involved.

"Yes… but you said—"

She shushed him, placing an index finger over her lips. "I know what I said, and it still stands, but who says we can't have some fun while we're at it?"

He nodded again. He could say nothing; there were no words to describe what he was feeling. He stood from the chair, walked over to the bed, and lay back, assuming what was supposed to be a nonchalant pose.

When Kallista reached him, she crawled onto the bed and over Sebastián until his face was right in front of hers. She lowered herself, straddling his manhood. He watched her breasts dangling delightfully and wished he could slide down enough to get his mouth on them. He reached to pull her up farther and heard her laugh.

"Easy there, tiger," she murmured as she wiggled out of his hands. She turned slightly to see he was still rock-hard, then faced him again with a smile. He was more than ready.

He pulled her up again, his eyes focused entirely on her breasts. He latched his mouth onto the right one, and she moaned with pleasure. Sebastián was eventually able to get her to a climax, and when she did, her back arched and she flung her head back, moaning loudly and grinding herself into him. During this erotic apogee, he sucked hard on her nipple and used some firm biting until her moans turned into a pleasure-induced scream.

She lay still on top of him for several moments, her hard breaths echoing off the furniture. She finally raised her head enough for them to see each other's faces, and he saw a satisfied twinkle in her eye.

"That was a pleasant surprise. You are very good with your mouth," she uttered with a smile.

"If you would allow me to make love to you, then you could—"

She shushed him once again, cutting him off. "I told you, I can't."

"Of course," Sebastián said. "I want only what you're comfortable with."

"Thank you, Sebastián."

She reached down, gently gripped his cock, and met his erection with her mouth. She kissed the head gently a few times while the other hand fondled his balls. Then, she shifted, and in one decisive movement, she slid her mouth over the head and down a sizable portion of his shaft.

"Oh, God!" Sebastián whispered as his eyes rolled back in ecstasy.

The pleasure was beyond words and beyond what he could have ever imagined. It felt as if he was rolling high on the waves of desire and sexual gratification without limits. He could stay there, in that spot, lost in her mouth forever. He no longer had even an ounce of doubt in his mind—this was the woman he wanted to be with the rest of his life. He would never let her go.

I am all yours, Kallista.

Sebastián reached up and slid his fingers into Kallista's hair, pulling away from the hair clip that held her hair back and watching as it cascaded down and around her face.

"Oh, Kallista!" he groaned. Kallista stroked his cock with her mouth in a slow, steady rhythm, sliding down on him and gliding back to the top. She moaned with him, heightening Sebastián's pleasure exponentially. She slobbered on his shaft, and things began to get a little messy but explosively erotic. He couldn't hold back any longer and shoved himself farther into her mouth.

As he became a more active receiver of the oral ecstasy she was delivering, she paused for a moment and smiled at him. In response, he picked up the pace until he was thrusting into her mouth with total abandon. She complimented his commitment to pleasure by increasing the amount of pressure she applied with her mouth. Sebastián was transported to a new level of happiness.

Don't stop, Kallista!

He had shut his eyes and tried to calm down to avoid climaxing too fast. He did not want Kallista to think he was a man who could not last more than a few minutes in bed. In the back of his mind, however, he wanted to go primal and slam himself into her mouth with all the strength he could muster then release every ounce of cum he had. He had never been so rough with a woman before, not even his first time many, many years ago as a teenager. At that moment, he no longer cared—and Kallista showed no signs of protest or displeasure.

He absorbed all the pleasure she gave him until he reached his climax, and his whole body exploded into the most powerful orgasm of his life. Dimly, he heard Kallista's soft moan of pleasure as she swallowed every drop of his cum. As the orgasm subsided, he opened his eyes and looked at Kallista. Something was different about her face. Her skin had changed, and her lips looked more luscious. Her skin glowed, and her eyes were brighter than they had been just a few moments ago.

"What's happening to you?" he asked as he pulled her up to wrap her in his arms.

"What are you talking about?" She had a confused look on her face.

He thought maybe he was going nuts for thinking his cum could make her look better.

"Nothing," he said hastily and tightened his arm around her, savoring the feeling of having her soft skin against his. But before he had a chance to get comfortable with her in his arms, things changed.

"I have to go," she said as she pushed his arms aside and got to her feet. She picked up her dress off the floor and slipped it back on. Sebastián also stood and put on a black silk robe as he walked toward Kallista. He did not want her to leave, now that they had, in his mind, consummated their relationship.

"Do you really have to go?"

"Yes, I do. I don't enjoy staying overnight at other people's houses."

"I am not *other people*, Kallista. I am Sebastián, and I love you. Please stay."

She smiled as if she knew something he did not. "I have to go. I will call you later."

There was no stopping her, but he had to keep trying. "Don't leave me, Kalli—"

She kissed him lightly on the lips, turned, and walked out without looking back.

It wasn't long before Sebastián heard her car start, then it faded away as she put more distance between her and his house.

41 | LAYLEN

"SHE HAS BEEN MEETING WITH a real estate agent she met at the lawyer's office. From everything we have been able to gather, it seems like she has a *thing* with him."

Laylen listened to Demetri as he gave his report, but there were things he knew about Kallista even before they started the surveillance mission. She would never get involved with a human because they were untrustworthy. When she walked out of the coven some forty years ago, it took a while before they noticed she was gone. They only realized when Jaqlyn needed Kallista's blood for an experiment to create purebloods.

Although his last conversation with Jaqlyn had not gone so well, she was calling him into the dome again to ask about his progress. "Do you not understand? She must want to come back and give herself willingly. That's the only way this can work! It's a critical part of the experiment, and without it, my experiment will not succeed."

"I am doing my best!" Laylen shouted. He knew immediately he'd made a mistake. He should not have yelled.

Jaqlyn turned on him and slapped him hard across the face, her eyes as dark as the depths of the sea. Instantly, the Gha'ueos in the other corner of the room ceased all conversation and stared in wide-eyed amazement at the two of them. Laylen looked at the vampire duo on the other side and saw that their astonishment matched his own.

He was lucky to have merely been struck across the face. Not once in his many years of service to Jaqlyn had she raised a hand to him. Even though the slap was not very painful, he knew how fortunate he was. Any other person would have been dead.

"You failed me! You have put a huge dent in my plans. I should never have trusted you with this. This was your great plan, to follow her around and just watch her until something comes up?"

"I believe it will work. I just need you to trust me!"

"Trust? Like I trusted you after the Holmium deaths? Trust is for fools, Laylen. Even you know this by now."

"I will get her here, I promise. I just need a little more time."

"This is your last chance, Laylen. If you don't come through soon, you are done! Do you understand?"

"Yes, I do."

He knew what she meant by *done*. A lot was riding on his success, but the most important of them was his life. Jaqlyn's patience was running out, and he could lose absolutely everything.

42 | KALLISTA

IT TOOK A LITTLE TIME, but George's properties and assets had been liquidated, and all the proceeds were now hers. However, this did not make her happy. Having that money felt like a weight tied to her feet. The money had become an ocean, and she felt like she was drowning. That much money didn't seem any better than having physical properties and assets. She would have to think of a way to rid herself of it to avoid the attention it was bound to attract.

A more pressing problem needed to be dealt with first. Sebastián had turned into an infatuated and overly needy man, and she had grown tired of him. The excitement she felt the first time they went out together was no longer there. But she was willing to give it another effort. So, she decided to give him a call.

"Hello."

"Bash, it's me."

"Hey, you."

"You feel like getting out tonight?"

"Sure, what do you have in mind?"

"The Ralworth Art Gallery."

Sebastián's response was hesitant. He wasn't one for art galleries, but anything to spend time with Kallista.

"Sebastián!" She called his name.

"I'm still here, Kallista. Sure, I would be happy to accompany you to the gallery. Pick you up in a bit."

"Okay, see ya soon."

Kallista knew he wasn't interested in going to the art gallery, but she wanted to make sure what they had was over.

Arriving at the gallery, it was early in the day and only a few cars were in the parking area. Once inside, Kallista was instantly intrigued with all the fabulous artwork;

Sebastián, not so much. He lagged behind, pretending to be amused. Kallista stopped in front of a painting of a woman sitting in front of a mirror.

"What's so special about this painting? What's the story?" Sebastián asked.

Kallista was annoyed by the questions. "It's art, Sebastián. Look at her. She is beautiful. It's a painting by an artist named Jules Enule Saintin. *Reflections.* You get the connection…" She stopped mid-sentence. A distinct aura was coming from across the room. She could feel the vibrations of energy given by this person; they were strong, in good health and balanced. This person had character and was regal.

She glanced over her shoulder to quickly scan the room and saw the beautiful anatomy of a man. His back toward her, he wore casual slacks with a tucked-in shirt and expensive dress shoes. Who was he?

"Kallista, Kallista!" Sebastián called out. "Where did you drift off to so suddenly? Are you alright? Do you know that person?"

"Nowhere, just caught up in thought. I'm fine, Sebastián, and no, I don't know that person. But I am ready to leave and go home alone." She needed to get rid of him.

They were at his lake house where he had convinced her to join him for a short getaway.

He stood at the window. A pair of tailored pants rode on his hips. He was just another ordinary man who had too quickly fallen in love with her physical attributes but never took the time to get to know who she was beneath her beauty. They were all in love with the look of perfection and obsessed with possessing that perfection. She was tired of superficial, one-dimensional guys.

"It'll be fun, Kallista," he had whined, insisting she joins him.

She also hated men who whined. She could feel herself becoming less attracted to him the more time they spent together. And she could feel him becoming more attached.

So here she was, locked in a lake house with a man who proclaimed to adore her. The more she thought about it, the more it bothered her and the more unbearable it became.

The night at the art gallery, the feelings she felt, she couldn't shake it, she needed to know more about this mysterious person.

"I want to go back home, Sebastián," she said, rising from the bed to slip into her robe.

"Why? It's so beautiful here."

"There are things I need to get back to," she said without making eye contact.

"You're a wealthy woman. You don't even have to work if you don't want to. What's so pressing you have to get back to?" He walked over to her from the window.

"Life!" she shouted.

"I love you, Kallista," he murmured gently, placing one palm on her cheek. "I would love nothing more than to prove it to you. I want to make love to you. I want to make you come again. We could be so happy together for the rest of our lives if you let me love you and give me your love in return."

Kallista knew he meant every word he said. He was starting to sound like George. And just like with George, his complete devotion to her was one-sided and only made things complicated and burdensome. It was time for her to make it simple once more.

"I want to have sex, but what do you think about me making you come multiple times?" she said with a mischievous grin on her face that suggested a promise of inexhaustible pleasure and unparalleled post-fellatio euphoria.

"That's a wonderful idea."

She smiled at his response. One moment, she was in his arms, and the next he was lying on the bed anticipating a good time. She pulled him closer to the edge of the bed and undid his fly. As usual, he was already hard. All she had to do was touch him, and he became engorged with desire. His passion transformed into pure animal lust and his body was beyond ready.

Kallista wetted her lips, still smiling. It had been four months since they'd met in Simon Wembley's office. She had hoped he would be different and not get attached, but just like George, Blake, and all the men before them who all became too clingy, he had to pay the ultimate price for his shallowness.

What good is a game if it always unfolded and ended the same way every time? It made the game monotonous and unfulfilling, and after so long, she didn't want to play anymore. She needed it to end now.

His cock engorged, and she could smell the delicious scent of his cum calling to her.

Humans often wished for a good death. For her, there was no such thing as a good death. There was death, and there was life. All deaths had the same result—the body turning into nothing more than meat and human consciousness disappearing. It was the ultimate end. Nevertheless, if she subscribed to the idea of a good death, she would say all the men she had killed had good deaths. They took the crossover from life to end immersed in the middle of pleasure and pain.

"I'd do anything for something salty to eat right now. Do you have anything salty for me?" Kallista asked with a grin. Without waiting for an answer, she said, "Oh, you do, do you?" She made a point to look at his penis for a brief second then returned her focus to his face. "Hmm… I may have something for you."

She stuck her tongue out and touched the tip of his cock where a large bead of pre-cum had already collected. She pulled her tongue back a little and sucked in the thin strand of cum. The taste was delectable as always.

She went back to teasing the head of his dick with her tongue, swirling it around the end at random speeds and directions. As Sebastián groaned, she could tell by his eyes and the look on his face he was aching to feel the warmth of her mouth. However, Kallista was not done teasing him yet. She slowly dragged the tip of her tongue down the length of his shaft before flattening her tongue to lick it like a lollipop on the way back up.

Her Nordic white hair shielded her face from his eyes, so she flipped it over to one side to make sure he had an unobstructed view before she finally opened her mouth and put his penis inside. She bobbed at the tip, stroking it with her tongue a few times before popping it back out. Licking up and down, all around as if she were licking an ice cream cone, all the while maintaining full eye contact with Sebastián. Her tongue darted up and down and across the tip, making Sebastián groan even more.

She could see in his face that his orgasm was already building from the combination of the oral action, the massaging of the shaft, and her beautiful face.

She inhaled deeply and took him in her mouth as deeply as she could, which sent Sebastián over the edge. He succumbed immediately and erupted as if it were his first time. She swallowed all he had to give, leaving nothing to waste. She continued to bob up and down as she took on more of his length. The head of his cock went past the back of her throat, but she managed to keep from gagging.

"Oh! Kallista!" he screamed.

Kallista pulled back a little to catch a breath, but she quickly got back on task and squeezed her lips around his cock to form a tight seal. This time, she used her tongue to dance at a sensitive spot at the base of his penis that, from her experience, was another means of drawing an intensified second orgasm. It worked perfectly. In a matter of minutes, she felt another powerful spurt at the back of her throat, and she smiled inside.

Kallista kept her now blood-orange eyes locked onto his half-closed eyes and held still as the cum passed into her mouth. As he mumbled how amazing she was between calling on God, Kallista wrapped her mouth around him and sucked harder, which rendered him multi-orgasmic with no apparent end in sight.

After the third wave passed, he managed to open his eyes and muttered with a sincere smile of complete satisfaction on his face, "Oh, Kallista! That was incredible! But that's enough for now." He tried to push her away, but she resisted and would not stop. Then the next wave hit.

After the fourth wave, finding his voice again, he demanded that she stop. "Kallista! Please stop!" he begged as he still tried to pull away. But stop, she did not. She kept going, and he kept cumming. Five orgasms. Six orgasms. Seven orgasms. Toward the end, and between orgasms, Kallista saw him struggle to speak, but all he managed was a look that pleaded for her to stop. Then his eyes slowly closed for their last time.

Kallista raised her head away from his now flaccid member and licked the remaining cum from around her mouth.

Sebastián was no more.

43 | LAYLEN

"SHE KILLED HIM!" BOTH VAMPIRES CLAMORED.

"How?" asked Laylen.

"I'm not sure. She didn't feed on his blood. When we found him, he was naked, and his cock looked bruised."

Laylen squeezed his face at that piece of information. "I can see you have a theory. What is it?"

Both vampires hesitated for a while. They had no idea how to tell Laylen what they thought happened to the human Kallista had been toying with for the past few months. "We think she sucked him to death."

Laylen grew impatient. "Didn't you just tell me she did not feed on him?"

"Yes, she did not feed on his blood. It appeared she might have fed on something else."

"What are you two saying?" he asked with clenched hands.

"She sucked his cock, and he orgasmed to death."

"What?" Laylen asked as he waited to hear the actual events of what happened. This was a joke. It had to be. Both vampires remained deadpan. "You're serious?" he asked as he realized they weren't joking.

"Yes, we are. The man was naked, lying face up on the bed, cock exposed, discolored and bruised, and there were none of the obvious signs of bloodletting such as pallor. It was the weirdest thing we have ever seen."

Laylen had no comments. He went to look at the body and verified the report for himself—Sebastián, indeed, still had blood in his body.

The questions were piling up, but he had no answers. None.

44 | DAVID

THURSDAY NIGHT AT 11:30 P.M., David Parham checked his cell phone impatiently, expecting a call from Osaka, Japan. He needed it to come through soon. The business deals he was working on had to be closed quickly so he could include the revenue earned in the current quarter's results.

He hated when his plans had to be altered. As a twenty-eight-year-old chief executive officer, he had learned the hard way that many things had to be done at certain times. Although he had finally made a name for himself and no longer had to prove himself to anyone, sometimes he still deemed it necessary. It was an essential part of who he was and how he became so successful. This, along with his self-esteem and confidence, was his most valuable attribute, and it kept him grounded when his opponents tried to knock him off his game. After all, the business world favored sharks.

At nineteen, he had dropped out of college and struck out on his own to start a think tank. Everyone thought he was crazy, but he knew he was on to something. He had a vision and had pursued it tirelessly. Eleven years later, he was one of the world's most influential entrepreneurs.

Many people believed in luck, but David didn't. He had always relied upon preparation, hard work, and self-confidence—and so far, this recipe had worked well for him.

By 12:30 a.m., he realized the call from Osaka was not going to happen. So, he retired for the evening but kept his phone close just in case.

After a good night's sleep, unfortunately, uninterrupted by any calls from Japan, he showered, dressed, and grabbed a light breakfast. He asked Greg, his chauffeur, to take him to the Ralworth Art Gallery on 88th street.

"Right away, sir."

He had been invited to an exclusive showing at the gallery. He had not planned to attend since he had just recently visited, but he unexpectedly found himself with free time on his hands and could think of no better distraction than the appreciation of artisanship.

The Ralworth Art Gallery, or the RAG as some of the younger crowd called it, stood against the sky majestically. Constructed mostly of white marble, it reminded David of the Taj Mahal. However, that was where the resemblance ended. Where the Taj Mahal reeked of pre-contemporary times, the Ralworth Art Gallery was modern. Clean lines and simplified forms lent to the present-day aura of the place. At first glance, the gallery looked like a trapezium with strategically situated show-glass in the middle that teased the onlooker's sense of wonderment, daring them to go in and view the marvels that lay therein. He appreciated the building's original architecture every time he visited.

"Ah, Mr. Parham! It's always a pleasure to see you!" the proprietor of the establishment, Harry Ralworth, exclaimed when he saw him.

"Always a pleasure to be here, Harry."

David Parham was the most revered client of the gallery. The artist they were exhibiting that evening was one with exceptional talent, so there was a good chance

David would spend a large amount of money on a few pieces of art that night.

The men shook hands, and David walked inside. There were only a few things in this world that excited him as much as discovering talented new artists. Art was an indulgence for him, but it was also a worthwhile investment opportunity. A piece from a new and promising artist could be worth a fortune in time. He had an eye for promising talent, but most of all, he had patience.

As he perused the various works of art on display, a piece caught his attention. It was as chaotic as it was brutal—it depicted the murder of a woman in all white by something that looked like a vampire. His interpretation of the piece was that it represented the death of innocence and beauty by life's ugliness. By a monster. It reminded him of his mother, the brutal attack that had taken her life and the day he went to Grimoir Arsenals.

It was the most pretentious name he had ever heard for a gun shop. The further he entered the store, the dustier the floor became. The state of the place surprised him. The floorboards creaked with every step, and there was peeling, fading paint everywhere he looked. What was designed to be vintage furniture had long become broken trash. In a corner, David saw chairs without legs and cabinets without doors—like a broken body with no soul. The air smelled old as if they had not opened the windows in a hundred years and that same old air had just been circulating and recirculating just as long.

He was on a mission to find something specific. He had paid wealthy for the information leading him here, but from the looks of the place, he was now very doubtful that this merchant would have anything near what he sought. On the wall behind an empty counter was the only sign that the store was in business. Hanging on the walls were many guns of various types, like a 9 mm handgun, but there were also shotguns and rifles. It was all very uninspiring.

The man with dark, steely eyes walked up to the counter. He looked like a person who had seen the deep-seated side of life too many times. David got straight to the point. "Someone told me I could purchase a certain blade here."

The man smirked, and it was loaded with secrets. It was the sneer that one would give a child asking about Santa Claus.

"And why do you want this blade?"

"Because I'm hunting a vampire."

"What do you know about vampires? They are characters of the stories we tell children to make them afraid of the dark."

David laughed, but it was devoid of joy or amusement. "I have seen the darkness with my own eyes. I watched as one of them took my mother's life. I was told I could find a vampire-killing blade here. So, do you have one or not?"

The man walked from behind the counter, walked over and locked the door, and put up the closed sign before walking past David again. As he passed him, he said, "Come with me."

They followed down a narrow hallway to the back of the store. The corridor led to a locked door. The owner opened it and they entered the large room. Inside, David saw an unusual set of weapons.

"I do have a blade, but not the type I think you want."

The man walked over to one side of the room and lifted a shiny silver blade.

"Silver doesn't work on them," David spat.

"This is not silver. It's a rare weapon made of Holmium. It's the only thing that can kill vampires."

"I want to buy it."

"It is not for sale. You must earn the honor of using it."

"Then that's exactly what I will do."

The man stared at him for a while as though he was trying to read his soul, then asked him to come back the following day.

There was no room for arguments or negotiating. David saw that the conversation on the blade was over for today. He was determined to lay his hands on that weapon. He agreed to return tomorrow, turned, and walked out of the room and out of the store.

"One must still have chaos within oneself to give birth to a dancing star," a female voice next to him said, banishing his preoccupation.

"Friedrich Nietzsche," he replied without taking his eyes off the painting.

"You know your philosophers," said the woman, standing beside him.

"Yes, I do. I have not…" His words trailed off when he saw who he was talking to. He had never seen her before, but he felt like someone had punched him in the gut. She was, for lack of a better word, exquisite. He was not a man to be blindly attracted to beauty, but her brand of beauty gave him pause. She was a living and breathing piece of art who had stolen his full attention.

They maintained eye contact without saying anything else. It lasted for what felt like a long time, but in reality, it was only a couple of seconds.

He struggled to reignite his line of thought, but it was awkward with her staring at him with those brilliant silver eyes. Finally, he remembered what he was going to say. "I have not…" but he stopped again and cleared his throat because his voice had become an embarrassing husky whisper. "I have not had the pleasure of being introduced to you," he finally said.

He looked composed even though he felt nothing of the sort.

"No, you have not. I'm Kallista."

"David Parham. It's a pleasure to meet you."

"The pleasure is all mine," she said and flashed him a smile, one that left him feeling like a giddy kid.

45 | KALLISTA

AS KALLISTA LOOKED UP AT the man, she not only felt a sunrise of pleasure unfurl within her, but that same aura she had felt the last time in the gallery. *Could it be him?* He was beautifully handsome—he had hazel eyes, a gorgeous smile with deep dimples, an even-toned dark complexion, and he was well-groomed. "Let me take a step back so I can get a better view of you," she said. It felt like he was towering over her five-foot-seven stature. He was the most striking man she had ever met, and although it was way too early to tell for sure, he seemed different. Where she was delicate, he was all hard male. His face had angles that qualified his handsomeness. It didn't take but a short while before she realized she wanted him.

If her hormones shifting to overdrive was not enough of a signal, the scent of his blood was. The smell of it and hearing it flow through his veins enticed her pallet. Reflexively, her fangs pushed at her gums, and it took all her effort to keep them in. She had never felt such an intense desire to fuck a man and drink his blood at the same time. Never.

David stared for another minute or so before he caught himself. "Do you know the artist?"

"No. But I'd heard of his work and decided to come check it out. I didn't have much to do and thought it would be a wonderful way to pass some extra time I had on my hands."

The unspoken truth was that she was remarkably familiar with the artist and equally fascinated by his work. She had seen one of the artist's old pieces in George's penthouse a long time ago. The painting amused her at first, but her amusement turned into intrigue when she recognized the building the artist painted. It was the dome of Zhovs.

No human artist could have painted the dome of Zhovs. The artist, therefore, had to be a vampire, and she became more than just a little curious to learn the artist's identity. George had gotten the painting through a private collector who, when she located him, swore he had never met the artist.

Imagine her surprise when she discovered the Ralworth Art Gallery was featuring that same artist's collection. She was excited to see other works of this artist, works that brought back many memories of her past.

"I am a connoisseur of the arts. I love anything that shows creativity, but some are exceptional. Some pieces can be so profound and soul-penetrating that it justifies and commands an exclusive exhibition such as this. And let's not forget the investment potential it could bring."

Kallista smiled at the way he passionately expressed his appreciation for fine art. She tried to imagine what it would feel like to have all that passion directed at her. She could, without a doubt, tell he was attracted to her by the flare of his nostrils and the dilation of his pupils as they interacted. But more so, she could smell the increased pheromones that spiced his blood only minutes after they first spoke.

It would be easy to get him to turn the passion on her. It was something she wanted. He had excited her without even trying, and she felt her body flush at the thought of his touch and the warmth of his skin. She had never had the urge to have actual sex with anyone, but this guy was different. She wanted him in every way possible.

"So, David, what do you do?"

"I own a company. You could call it a research institute of sorts where we bring experts together to conduct research and advocate topics like social policy, political strategy, economics, military, technology, culture… You name it, we research it."

"You own a think tank?"

"Yes, exactly. I must say I'm impressed. Not a lot of people know exactly what a think tank does."

"Well, how could I not know? The way you described… it sounds like the Merriam Webster verbatim definition of a think tank."

"Of course, it is. It was my office that virtually standardized the think tank definition online."

Kallista laughed. "Wait… You're David Parham."

"Yes."

"You own Parham Incorporated?" she asked as the name clicked.

"Yes, I do."

"I didn't think you'd be so young," Kallista said with an expression close to admiration. She did not regard many humans, but David Parham was doing a fantastic job at winning her approval.

"Most people don't," he said with all seriousness.

"Yes, I bet they assume the owner will be an older man in his fifties or sixties with a pouch, receding hairline, and wrinkles everywhere."

"Exactly!"

They both burst out in a warm, comfortable laughter spiced with moments of heart-racing nervousness. Together, Kallista and David walked across the length of the gallery looking at other pieces by the featured artist.

Soon, Kallista forgot all about the artist and became engrossed in David's essence and his stories. She was no longer interested in anything else but him.

The evening ended earlier than she wanted.

"Can I give you a ride home?" David asked as they walked out of the gallery together. She felt like she had known him all her life.

Mate.

The word was as dangerous as it was exciting. She would never forget all the times Jaqlyn had told her that having a mate would be the end of her.

They make you weak, leave you exposed, and before you know it, you're gasping for breath. Struggling to hold on to the life that is being taken from you. You're left open with nothing. I have seen it happen to vampires before, seen them become a shadow of themselves because they were stupid enough to fall in love. Never let it happen to you.

"No, I came in my car," she said as she pushed the thought of Jaqlyn's admonishment out of her head.

After they reached her car, David said, "Good night, Kallista," as he opened the door for her like a true gentleman.

"Goodbye, David. Be safe getting home."

"Thanks. You too."

The rest of the night went well over into the next one. Kallista could not stop thinking about David. However, she decided that it would be best not to see him again. She had forgotten all about the artwork she went to see. She concluded the artist was another vampire who had gone rogue and established himself among humans. The artist and David were no longer relevant, so for the sake of her heart, she made a vow to herself that she could not and would not see David Parham ever again.

46 | KALLISTA

IT HAD BEEN FOUR WEEKS since Kallista was at the gallery. Four weeks since she met the man that excited her in so many undiscovered ways. The excitement was an emotion she was not familiar with. She knew fury, she understood bloodlust, and she was even familiar with lust to a limited extent, but excitement… that was foreign. She felt the way she imagined a drug addict would feel if he didn't get his fix at the right time. Jittery and out of sorts, she was finding it increasingly difficult to focus on anything besides David.

David had hijacked her thoughts to the point that she had not even fed in days. She could already see the signs when she looked in the mirror—a gaunt look was starting to show on her face, baggy eyelids, crows' feet, and lackluster hair, making her look decades older.

I must feed.

It was time for her to hunt. Even though she wanted to be careful enough to feed but not kill, she could not be sure of what she would do until she had her fangs buried in her prey.

For this hunt, and with her vampire quickness, she went to the seedier part of town. It was filled with underprivileged and outcasts, humans who no one would search for if they went missing.

That night she saw a man in a poorly lit area of an abandoned playground. When she saw what he was doing, she realized he was a human monster. Kallista found him kneeling over a young lady's body, and the scent of blood filled the air. Whoever she was, she did not deserve to die like that—he had stabbed her repeatedly and was still stabbing her.

"Whore," he repeatedly whispered as he continued. Even though it was clear she had already died, he continued stabbing.

Kallista walked out of the shadows and up to him. He whirled around when he felt her presence.

"Why did you kill her?"

"Who the fuck are you?" He leaped to his feet and pointed the knife at Kallista with a startled look on his face.

"Why did you kill her?" Kallista repeated as she took a step closer.

"I said, who the fuck are you? It doesn't matter. You have no business here." Still pointing the knife at Kallista's throat, he said, "Now you're gonna die too, bitch!"

"Am I?" Kallista asked with her hands folded behind her back.

He swung at her with the knife but missed when she swerved to his other side. It happened so fast, he didn't even see her move.

"What the hell?" He looked left then right, trying to find where she'd gone. After locating her, he turned to face her again, bewildered, with his eyes wide open and an unsteady knife pointed at her.

She smiled at him and let her fangs show. She could smell the fear pouring out of him. "What's wrong, little man? You seem afraid."

"What are you!?"

"Your damnation!" she said as she closed the distance between them, grabbed him by his neck, and lifted him off his feet with one hand. Usually, when she fed, the experience was pleasurable for her prey. But in this loser's case, she unleashed terror on him. She slammed him to the ground and was all over him with a quickness. She buried her fangs in his neck and gulped his blood. She kept her hand over his mouth, so his muffled screams didn't travel. He tried thrashing to get her off him, but his elevated heart rate coupled with Kallista's swift exsanguination made death come quickly.

When he was no more, she stood over him, stared at his lifeless body, and kicked it just because. The young lady he had attacked already had the pallor of the dead, so there was nothing she could do for her. But it didn't matter, because she was no vigilante. In fact, she was a monster in her own right too.

As she was about to walk away, she stopped and looked down at the dead woman. "The world is filled with monsters like me. I wished you would have learned to recognize us."

Her thirst for blood had been sated, yet she walked away, feeling empty. She was still in need of something to divert her mind, and after a few seconds, she visualized the right place to do so.

The gallery.

She would go back to the gallery and view that painting again, even buy it if it was still available. That way, every time she stared at it, she could reminisce about the tall man with the hazel eyes that made her heart race. She returned home to clean up and change her clothing.

When she arrived at the gallery in her Aston Martin, she valet-parked and walked inside. The gallery looked different from the night she had been there with David. It was quieter without a lot of patrons or the clinking of champagne flutes. She stood in front of the piece and tilted her head as she studied it closer.

"Interesting piece, yes?"

Kallista stared at the man she recognized to be the proprietor of the gallery.

"Yes, remarkably interesting. How much is it?"

"The asking price is two million dollars," he replied.

"I'll take it," she said without the slightest hesitation.

"Yes, of course." With a muted smile, he added,

"Excellent choice, ma'am. I will get things started for your purchase."

"I have been searching all over for you," David said when she walked out of the gallery.

The shock was plastered on Kallista's face as she now regretted her decision of going there. However, it was too late. She was there already, and now he was there, and her heart started racing again. She continued walking down the stairs in his direction. The black high-rise trouser pants and form-fitting top she had on made her look modest and chic. He wore a simple T-shirt with a pair of jeans and Sperry's.

"Have you now?" she asked, trying hard to sound nonchalant about his unexpected appearance. She failed—her voice came out sounding breathless and filled with tension.

"Yes, I have." He reached out for her hand.

"How did you find me?"

"A little bird told me," he said with a wink of an eye.

Kallista laughed and retorted, "More like a big bird that goes by the name of Harry Ralworth."

"Pardon him. I have been going crazy, trying to find you. I made him promise to call me if you ever come back."

Kallista and David stared at each other for a moment. It felt like coming home.

Love perhaps?

It was not meant to be instantaneous, not like that, but she had developed a link to this man that no other emotion could explain. It was strange and a little silly, but it was what it was.

"Can I drive you home?" he asked. She said yes, forgetting she had driven herself there.

"Great. So, what were you doing in the gallery?" he asked as they walked toward his car, hand in hand.

"I bought that strange piece with the woman in white."

"The piece?" he asked with surprise as he opened the car door for her.

"Yes, the piece," she said, looking at him as she slid into the car.

"Turn here," Kallista said as they drove up the long driveway to her house. "We're here."

He stopped the car in front of her delightful looking house. "Why do you live so far away from the city? This place is so secluded."

"I don't like neighbors," she answered with a smile and a shrug.

"Wow, really? That's not safe. There are a lot of dangerous things out there."

"You're right." She could hear the concern in his voice, and it amused her. "But don't you worry. I know how to take care of myself."

David smiled. "I'm sure you do."

Kallista smiled back but stiffened when he leaned in to give her a friendly kiss on the cheek. It was strange to have a man give her such an innocent kiss these days. Any other man would have tried to at least cop a feel—with ulterior motives to have sex with her as soon as they had her alone.

"May I have your number so I can call you next week once I return from my business trip? Perhaps we can set dinner plans."

Kallista let out a candid laugh which was her way of expressing the joy she felt at that moment. Laughing felt so surreal that when the laughter came out, she knew she had not been living at all, only existing. She felt alive in a way that nobody had ever made her feel. It was glorious, and she wanted to keep feeling this way forever. She no longer felt like the killing machine her mother had turned her into. Neither did she feel like the heartless monster that went around murdering infatuated men. She felt different, a good different.

"Dinner sounds great," she said with a smile while she continued her enthusiasm.

She gave him her phone number and watched him drive away. Jaqlyn had it all wrong when it came to love, and Kallista would prove it.

47 | KALLISTA

SHE WENT THROUGH HER CLOSET more times than she cared to admit, searching for the right outfit. The nervousness that assailed her was strange. She had never obsessed over what to wear on a date. However, this was not a regular date. It was a date with David, and she wanted to impress him.

Finally, she shook herself and decided to go with a royal blue dress that looked wonderful against her skin tone. She aimed to look stunning but with a touch of class to complement David's refinement and charm.

Her phone rang as she stepped out of the bathroom. It was David. Hearing his voice made her instantly happy and jittery at the same time. He had returned home from his trip that morning, and they had already set their dinner date for that evening.

"Kallista." The way he pronounced her name made her insides turn to jelly.

"Hello, David."

"I'm almost at your home," he said.

"I'm almost ready. See you in a bit."

"See you soon."

She felt euphoric. And that night, one would be hard-pressed to find a more beautiful woman who was as well-dressed as her.

"Wow! You look mind-blowing," David said as soon as she let him in. He took in the decor of her home and smiled with approval. He glanced at the artwork she'd bought in the gallery. It sat on the floor next to the marble mantle. The look on his face gave away the fact that the picture was not one he would have chosen. But he shifted his attention back to Kallista as she spoke.

"Thank you, David. You look wonderful too. I'm ready," she said.

He took her hand as they walked out of the house to his car.

"Somehow, I get the feeling you don't like the piece."

David looked at her for a moment. "You're very observant," he said with another smile.

She noticed he grinned a lot when they were together.

"So…why don't you like it?"

"I'll tell you after dinner."

They settled into a comfortable silence at the dinner table, and Kallista was grateful for it. She needed time to process what she wanted to do, but more specifically, how far she wanted to take this thing with David. Being with him made her realize she had been alone for far too long. She always had a man in her life, but she hadn't connected with any of them the way she did David.

He smiled at her, and she smiled right back.

"This place is beautiful," Kallista said as she looked around again.

"I'm glad you like it."

The Nocturne restaurant in the River North District of Denver was well-appointed with none of the gaudiness that many men seemed to think would impress a woman. Instead, it radiated style, elegance, and sophistication—just like the man in her company.

It had been a long time since she ate a decent human meal, but the dinner tonight was over-the-top amazing. She had the chili lime steak with roasted vegetables. And for dessert, she chose the chocolate mousse topped with sweetened whipped cream and bittersweet chocolate shavings.

When they finished their meal, they talked about whatever came to mind—from family, hopes, and aspirations, to philosophy, economics, and life lessons learned. They sat for a long while chatting and giggling over glasses of wine until it was just the two of them left in the restaurant.

It was the most fun Kallista had ever had.

48 | DAVID

DAVID PARHAM WAS SMITTEN.

He had found the one for him.

"I had an amazing time Kallista," he said when they got into the car.

"So did I. I enjoyed myself."

"We talked about so many things, I never got around to answering your question about the painting. It reminds me of a dark time in my life. My mother… well, um, she was killed before my eyes," he said.

"Oh my! I'm sorry to hear that. What happened, if you don't mind me asking?"

"No, I don't mind. A monster killed her while I sat helplessly and watched. That painting reminds me of the night she died. It was spring, and the flowers that had been a tight bud only days ago had begun to open and display their deeper blush of pink. Winter—a mild one—had ended several weeks ago, but spring had already begun to push temperatures to a comfortable level. There was even a gentle breeze blowing as Mother and I walked into the park. After we found a bench and settled in it, I went to go touch the flowers. That's when I saw Amanda and forgot all about the flowers. Amanda was a good friend of mine. We had known each other for a few years. She and I were both twelve and shared a few classes together at school. My mother just sat on the park bench and chatted with a man I didn't recognize.

"Amanda and I sat on the swings and talked until she had to leave. After she had gone, I went back toward the bench where my mother had been sitting, but she was no longer there. I looked around, thinking I may have gone to the wrong bench, but I couldn't find her. I walked around and yelled out for her, but she didn't answer. She was nowhere to be found. That's when I realized that I was the only one left in the park. I yelled even louder for her, but still, there was no answer. I had already started to panic, and after about ten minutes of searching, the park lights came on. I heard something, a scuffling sound behind a large bush of flowers near where mom had been sitting.

"As I walked toward the noise, I continued to call for my mom. As soon as I rounded the flowers, the first thing I noticed was a pair of red eyes. Fear seized my voice—there was a monster in the bushes. It had my mother pinned against a retaining wall with its mouth fastened onto her neck.

"I must have made a sound, a whimper, or something because it looked directly at me. This beast was the man I saw talking with my mother earlier on the park bench. Even though it saw me, the monster didn't stop feeding. Then, as if it had been waiting for me, it ripped my mother's neck open. I stood and watched in horror as her eyes turned to nothingness.

"'Mom!' I screamed. With two long fangs that extended down the corners of its mouth, the monster smiled and took off so fast I thought I was dreaming. My mother crumpled to the ground when it let her go. In time, I realized the monster was a vampire."

"I'm sorry, David. I am," Kallista said.

He tightened his hand around hers, and they rode to her house without saying a word.

At the end of that night, David Parham knew he wanted Kallista in his life forever. He was a man who knew how to keep his eyes on the prize, and Kallista was his prize. He looked forward to spending more time with her at his house, and it seemed she was comfortable with that idea. His space would become their space.

49 | JAQLYN

"TELL ME YOU HAVE SOMETHING," Jaqlyn said with blazing eyes.

Every other thing was in place. The coven was booming, and their businesses in the human world were raking in non-stop cash flow.

For a millennium, they had remained secluded and protected from the human world, especially after the Holmium deaths. But Jaqlyn convinced the coven that the world was a changed place. The Zhovs needed to trade with the humans to thrive. Therefore, vampire artists sent out their works to be auctioned off. And the mystery behind the origins of their artworks made them highly valued. They also invested in the stock market, which resulted in very handsome returns on their vested interests.

Even though the coven was doing fine, Jaqlyn still needed Kallista to create the serum that would make the vampires immune to Holmium. She had changed her short-term aim from creating purebloods from birth to turning the vampires on the ground into ones resistant to sunlight and Holmium. In time, she would resume her original goal to find a breakthrough in creating purebloods. But as for now, harnessing Kallista's immunity was a more pressing objective. The problem was, and remained, she could not abduct her. Kallista had to walk into the coven on her own and donate her bone marrow under her own free will for the procedure to work.

Laylen stood straight and stared at her with confidence written all over his face.

"I do have something," he said.

"Tell me." She smiled grimly, her arms crossed.

"Kallista has been spending much of her time with a certain man. And from all indications, I believe she has fallen in love."

Jaqlyn scoffed.

"Love? That girl learned nothing!" she spat with disgust.

Laylen kept quiet, watched, and waited.

"What does that have to do with anything?"

"I believe if we seize the man she has fallen in love with and bring him here, she will willingly come back to the coven to save his life. Will that work?" he asked with a touch of weariness creeping in his tone.

A smile spread across Jaqlyn's face. "Yes, I think that will do. All that matters is that she walks into the laboratory on her own. She is a creature of magic and can't be made to do anything against her will. But as long as it is her will to come here, the procedure will be successful. Agreeing to be a part of my experiment will be the price for his release."

Laylen smiled. His job was ending, and he smelled victory for himself.

50 | KALLISTA

KALLISTA AND DAVID HAD BEEN together for close to two years now, she controlled her bloodlust and her aging appearance hidden. She ate a light diet whenever she and David were together. This called for her to take an occasional evening away from David to feed and sate her bloodthirst.

Being kind is a terrible idea. It is best to be ruthless.

That was what Jaqlyn had taught her. It was also the only lesson she took away from her mother. Even though she feared love, she knew she had already fallen for David. He was turning her entire world upside-down and had changed her life in ways she never imagined possible. It was the most fantastic thing that had ever happened to her.

Every single time she saw him, it felt as if space and time became the most delicate point conceivable. Now every thought and every feeling she had led right back to his heart and soul—he was her home. Her love for him was real. So real it eclipsed her underlying fear.

David differed from all the men she had been with. He treated her with the utmost respect and adoration. He showed interest in everything about her. And he never asked to have sex. That alone had astonished her. She felt valued and never wanted to lose that feeling. At the same time, she increasingly wanted him to be her first. She fantasized over and over about the day she would feel his cum streaming down her throat, his penis inside of her. Sex with him would be a spiritual union, one long overdue.

One night while sitting together at the dinner table by the flickering glow of candlelight, the remnants of the meal sitting on the plates before them, Kallista placed her palm on David's cheek and asked, "Why don't you ever touch me… sexually?"

"Touch you?"

"Yes, apart from the innocent kisses on the cheek. You have never tried to kiss me with a sense of passion."

"Kallista, that's because I love you and I respect you too much to take advantage of you."

"But, David, I *want* you to touch me. Anywhere you want, any way you desire. I just don't want you to touch anybody else."

He got up from his chair, walked to her side, took her hand, and gently bid her to stand. After she stood, he tightened his arms around her and pressed his lips against hers. After the real kiss, he looked her in the eyes with the most serious look on his face she had ever seen. "You are mine, Kallista," said David. "And I am all yours."

Mine.

This word resonated in her head. It felt right to be his, and she realized at that moment, he wouldn't let her go no matter what. David took her lips in a fierce kiss, branding her. The embrace, the kiss, the love, and the moment were seared into her brain.

As he kissed her, the world fell away. His hands gently touched her ears, and his thumbs caressed her cheeks as their breaths mingled. Kallista ran her fingers down his back, pulling him close enough to feel the beating of his heart against her chest.

"I am a virgin," she whispered to him soon after he released her.

His eyes widened, then he kissed her forehead. "You do not understand how happy that makes me," he muttered.

It was a strange reaction. All the other men were disheartened when she told them. "I want to please you in so many ways," she said with a smile meant to seduce.

David laughed aloud as if she had said something amusing. "No, no. I respect you, Kallista. I love you, and I want you so much, but I would prefer to wait until we are married." Kallista's eyes widened. "Yes, I want to marry you."

"I love you," she responded, even though she could not wrap her head around the concept of marriage and its importance to humans.

She let her guard down when they were together. She had been so caught up in him; she had been eating human food since they met for the sake of appearance. The last time she fed on blood was several months ago.

Suddenly, her attention was redirected as she heard the blood roaring through the arteries in his neck. First, her heartbeat increased, and a powerful and unhinged urge soon followed, which she fought as hard as she could to keep it from consuming her very being. But as hard as she tried, the urge won, and all she wanted now was to feed.

Her fangs pushed through her gums, projecting out of her mouth in a readiness to partake what had become a new and delicious source of food. She could smell his blood beneath the skin, and it was intoxicating.

No! This is David! I can't do this!

With every ounce of strength and fortitude she could draw up, she fought her basic impulse and suppressed her hunger.

David, unaware of her inner struggle, moved closer to embrace her. "I love you, Kallista," he whispered.

She had always longed for love as intense as her desire to feed. Now she had love, but it only intensified her hunger, given she had been without blood for so long. The bloodlust replaced her meditations, and it was building vigorously. She did all she could to keep it at bay and under some level of control. But she could no longer manage.

At last, it took over her entire soul. The fight was over. Every ounce of self-control she had was now gone.

She succumbed to her natural desires. Her silver eyes turned blood-orange. Her body tensed slightly.

He cannot see me like this! He won't understand!

Still, she hoped he would.

David raised his head. "What's wrong?"

She gave him no response. He pulled away to look at her. Her hair was no longer Nordic white—it was now bright amber red.

"Please! Please! Wait! David!" she called out to him, but he was lost in a world of his own. He could no longer see her. "Please look at me, David!"

Her heart was riddled with grief, crashing in like waves in a hurricane. She could not wrap her head around it completely. Death would feel more pleasant than this pain of losing David's love and affection.

"David, listen!" she screamed, but he was too far gone and lost in some psychotic haze. "I am a vampire. This is what I do. I have ruined the lives of many people. I have destroyed families. And I have killed without a second thought to survive. But David, since I met you, I have changed."

The painful truth choked the breath from her body and short-circuited her mind. What was once whole was now shattered. David didn't look at her, he tried to keep focused. He stormed away angrily. David continued on his unknown mission through his house in search of something, she stumbled after him, trying to plead her case. But he was still not receptive to her. He had a desperate look on his face.

When she was close enough, she reached out and grabbed the tail of his shirt and said, "I am not the monster you think I am, David. I love you, and I will always do what's best for you and what's best for us. I would never harm you, but this is who I am. I was once proud and strong, but if you take your love from me now, all that would be left of me would be shattered fragments that would never make me whole again. Please, don't be afraid of me. I love you too much to hurt you. Just stop what you're doing and hold me in your arms. Please! And never let me go."

He paid no mind to her. Instead, he freed himself from her grip and ran into his room. Kallista followed him with tears in her eyes, still fighting hard to stop the bloodlust. She was fighting a battle she couldn't win, and despite her words, she wanted nothing more than to bury her fangs in his neck and drink from him. But not to kill him—he was the love of her life and her chosen mate.

"David! Please! Let's talk about this!"

51 | DAVID

WHEN DAVID LOOKED INTO KALLISTA'S eyes, he didn't recognize the woman who stood before him. His body froze, his mouth agape. He no longer saw Kallista; he now saw was the monster from his childhood that killed his mom. His mind decompensated and became that scared little boy again.

You cannot buy a blade without knowing how to use it, the store owner had said to him all those years ago.

Now he had found his monster, it was time to put that knowledge to practical use and make it pay for killing his mother.

The blade.

While in his bedroom looking, he recalled it was in his study, in the bottom drawer of his desk. If he could reach it, he could kill the monster now in his house and send the demon back to hell.

He stumbled through the house as the evil feign kept following him. He had to get to it as fast as possible. He cut through the bathroom and out the other door and ran to his study. He had to hasten to put more distance between him and this creature.

"There you are!" he heard behind him as he was running. Then the sound of her footsteps following in his direction. Without looking back, he said with violent and uncontrolled anger, "You betrayed me, Kallista!"

After making it into his study and retrieving the blade, he realized the monster was saying something. He had to be careful, or it would see what he had. He would have to be cunning to ensure his plan worked. He had trained extremely hard for a long time, waiting for a moment like this. He would not let this blood-sucking demon get away.

The monster had tried to fool him, but he understood its tricks. He knew monsters did not always display their pure forms. Sometimes they wore a human-like mask to disarm people into lowering their guard. But it prepared him to defend his kind from having to live through the loss of a loved one by monsters like her. Or he would die trying.

52 | KALLISTA

"PLEASE! LISTEN!" KALLISTA SAID AS she faced David's back. She remembered all the men who had also begged for her affection, men she had killed without remorse. It was a dam sealed a long time ago by her mother's training, but it had taken true love to unlock her human nature.

"I am so sorry!" she sobbed as she approached him from the back. Tears trailed down her cheeks for the first time in her life. Despite her pain, she couldn't help but curse Jaqlyn for making her suppress her humanity. Now, for the first time, she felt her humanness would become one of her greatest strengths.

You were wrong, Mother. My humanity is a gift.

But as she reached David, he whipped around with the Holmium blade in his hand. She recognized it, but it was too late to respond or react. Questions flashed across her mind, none of which would get an answer.

In one fluid move, he drove the blade straight into her heart. The pain was exquisite and radiated through her entire body as she fell to the floor.

Even though the level of pain she was experiencing was excruciating, the sensation was foreign to her, and in some crazy way, she enjoyed it. As she lay on her back with her life force spreading across the cold floor, a smile appeared on her face. The pain had turned into numbness now.

He must have practiced this before, she thought to herself, trying to justify the speed and expertise in which David had used the blade.

Then, she remembered his words, and it all made perfect sense.

A monster killed my mother, and I saw everything. No one believed me.

A vampire had killed his mother, that was why he learned how to kill vampires. She felt tears stream down her face at the thought of this. After the life she had lived and the many men she had killed under similar circumstances, she was now dying at the hands of the love of her life. Holmium would not kill her as it did regular vampires, but the blade had been driven deep into her heart. The Holmium.

What an irony.

53 | DAVID

DAVID LOST IN THE HAZE. He stared at the creature on the floor with exasperation. *The blade should have turned it to dust, so why is it still whole?*

Then he remembered what the store owner had told him all those years ago. *Vampires are a tricky lot,* the store owner had said. *They are trying to find ways to build resistance to Holmium, so do not be surprised if you meet one that does not die at the touch of the blade. Be sure to drive the edge into its heart then cut it into pieces. It's not enough to drive the blade in if they do not immediately turn to ash. They can and will recuperate and come back to haunt you. You must cut them into pieces as soon as you have the chance.*

"Pieces. Pieces. Pieces," David chanted as he removed the Japanese Katana he had hanging on the wall.

Most people over the years thought the sword was decorative and just for show when in fact the sword was there for this specific purpose.

After he drew the sword, he did not think twice about it before bringing it down on Kallista repeatedly with all his might. Her blood spurted from her body and splattered over the walls, furniture, and floor. Each time he brought the sword down, he could hear metal cutting through bone, and even cutting through to the floor. But he continued. It had only taken one blow to sever her head, but when he did, it rolled away from her torso to the other side of the room.

He hacked at her body until there were body parts scattered all over and sitting in blood. Exhaustion etched across his face. But he continued. He had become lost to the madness that had engulfed him like fire and had unleashed his psychosis. With every swing and every cut, his sane mind disintegrated even farther until David Parham, the person, was no more. He was replaced by the repressed version of himself that was born that night in the park when he lost his mother to a monster.

54 | LAYLEN

"DID YOU HEAR THAT?" LAYLEN ASKED.

"Yes," said Taylor.

"She lost her mind," he muttered from the bushes where they kept watch.

"This is the perfect time to get her. She is vulnerable. It will be easier to manipulate her now."

"We cannot manipulate her. She must come of her own free will."

The other two were fully aware of the extent of Kallista's power, but Laylen knew something was wrong. If she was indeed in trouble, rescuing her might make her feel indebted to him. It was the perfect time to make a move.

"Let's go!"

They hurried with a stealth that was second nature to them. However, secrecy had become useless in the face of what they saw looking in through the window. Everything in the world seemed to slow, and it was as if all sound was distorting through an ocean of water. Laylen was in shock and unable to move a muscle as he stared at the man hacking away at Kallista's body.

Then, at some unconscious level, and with a roar borne of pain, he was suddenly at the man's throat. There was madness in his eyes. Without any hesitation or forethought, Laylen dug his fangs wide into David's Adam's apple and ripped his throat out.

55 | DAVID

DAVID NEVER SAW IT COMING. He did not see the three vampires in his window as he continued to kill his monster. He did not even notice when one of those vampires was suddenly beside him, followed by what sounded like a roar. And David never saw, and never would have imagined—even in his right mind—what happened next. He was about to serve another blow when the vampire grabbed him, pulled his head back, sank his fangs deep into his neck, and ripped out his throat in the fraction of a second.

Clutching what remained of his throat in his hands and with blood flowing through his fingers, he fell to the floor with horror-filled eyes. Then came a moment of clarity. He would share the same fate as his mother. Damn vampires.

He tried to gasp for breath, but he drowned in his own blood. In the last moment of his life, David Parham smiled. He was going home.

56 | LAYLEN

"FUCK!" LAYLEN SCREAMED AFTER DAVID took his last breath.

He did not want to rehash the prospect of informing Jaqlyn of his failure. The most pressing question now was whether he might have lost the chance to redeem himself with her. He also wondered if she would ever forgive him for not saving Kallista.

57 | JAQLYN

"WHAT IS THIS?" JAQLYN ASKED, eyeing the blood-soaked bag Laylen placed before her.

"Your daughter."

Stepping away from the throne, Jaqlyn opened the bag and gasped. The haughty little girl was gone. In her place was a pile of body parts and blood.

"Take it to the lab," she mumbled. "Happy birthday, child."

There was a story here, but she was not interested in hearing it. Perhaps someday she would be ready, but at that moment, Jaqlyn battled with several emotions.

Chief amongst them was regret.

ACKNOWLEDGMENTS

EVERYDAY WRITING IS HARD ENOUGH. Writing about a story you have conjured up in your mind is even harder. I could not have completed this book without the help of so many others. Many thanks to all of those who worked on bringing this story of Kallista to fruition. Thank you for your patience, time, advice, suggestions and for your understanding. Much credit to all for such magnificent work—credit me with the rest.

My editors, Michelle Rascon (EditorRascon.com), Kit (kit56) Duncan (fiverr), and Dara "editor Dara" Dumilola. My beta reader, Luis Andrepres. My cover designer, Flora "Flori" Figueroa (Fiverr), who I often challenged throughout the process but remained with me until the end—much appreciation for all her patience, going beyond, and creating my vision.

Kimolisa for great formatting.

As always, I acknowledge my Lord and Savior for everything big and small.

My family, thank you for your patience endurance and putting up with me as I was busy writing. Thank you for always being my biggest crowd, my cheerleaders. Thank you for believing in me always. And to my significant other Earl for being so accepting and willing to take the time out of his busy schedule to help with revising the story from a man's point of view. I love you all.

I am joyed and proud to have finally finished the book. It took strength, understanding, determination and much patience.

ABOUT THE AUTHOR

Do one thing every day that scares you.

–Eleanor Roosevelt

just Deirdre was born in New Orleans, Louisiana and grew up in Kansas City. Since then, she moved around until finally settling in Alabama. She has been in a long-distance relationship with her significant other for 20 years. Deirdre has three adult children, five grandchildren, and one grand dog.

Class of 1981 graduate from FL Schlagle High, Deirdre was a single parent and worked hard to provide for her family. At 40, she attended Strayer University, where she obtained a master's degree in business administration.

Under the pseudonym **Petite Breaux**, Deirdre has written a memoir *Slightly Bruised and a Little Broken*, a short story *The Whispering of My Heart* and a children's book *Fun with Grandma*. She has recently released several short stories, a suspense novel and currently working on her final novel The Journal, Nancy Bremen Story, to be released late 2019 under the name **just Deirdre**.

When she gets the time and has the inclination, Deirdre enjoys exercising at her local gym. She loves watching TV and movies and goes to the theater when there is something that grabs her attention. She also reads daily and is learning the guide of meditation to rejuvenate the soul.

Deirdre also enjoys getting away from it all on vacation, with cruising as her favorite pastime. She has plans to live her best life to the max and has done some of the things that scare her like ziplining and parasailing. She also plans to do a skydive one day.

In the future, Deirdre wants to make more time for her family, travel, and write books that will entertain across generations.

You can contact just Deirdre or follow her at:

Website: https://www.petitebreaux.com

Email: petitebreaux@yahoo.com

Twitter: https://twitter.com/AuthorPetiteB

Facebook: https://www.facebook.com/petitebreaux

Please Review

I hope you enjoyed reading Kallista, The Forbidden One as much as I enjoyed writing it. Of course, I would appreciate a brief review on Amazon, Goodreads, or one of your other favorite online book retailers. Just one line could make a difference as reviews are crucial for authors to be successful, particularly us indie authors.

ALSO, BY just Deirdre.

Short Stories:

Derek and Camella, Homegirl Misled

Samson and Taylor, Cruise Interrupted

Clyde and Ginger, When Love Isn't Enough

Young and Reckless, New Faces

Sought Out, Online Hookup

Pest of a Bug, Work Humor

Novels:

Something Inside: Fiction/Suspense

The Journal, Nancy Bremen Story: A novel,

Fiction/Drama/Abuse

Here is a special reader preview

of my 2019 new release

THE JOURNAL, NANCY BREMEN STORY.

Will be available in Ebook, paperback and hardback. Get

your copy and please leave a review.

Chapter 1

ALL MY LIFE, I associated funerals with rainy days. Momma's funeral should not have been on such a sunny day. The irony of that bright, cheery day was not lost on me, even at nine. Birds chirped louder than ever. The sun shone down from her apex. The service passed in a blur of sadness and sheer boredom. When the formalities were over, Grandma Ivie remained seated, so did my twin brother Brian and me.

A tall man with speckled gray hair on both sides of his head ambled towards us. Salt and pepper, Momma called it. Calmly, he kneeled in front of us. In his mid-thirties, he looked about the same age as Momma. He wore a coat, even though it was a little too hot for it. He looked tired, his attire a little shoddy for a funeral. It was as if he'd come from far away and wasn't planning to stay long.

He spoke in a gentle but indifferent tone. "I am sorry for your loss; your momma was a great woman and mother." Then he kissed us both on the forehead and rose to his feet. "Take care of them," he said, avoiding eye contact with Grandma Ivie.

"That's it, Daniel?" she asked, incredulous, her voice raw with emotions. I remember her voice shaking a little as she spoke, the same way Momma's did when she didn't want to break down. "Am I supposed to take care of them? What about you? They just lost their mother, the only parent they had. Don't you have a responsibility here?"

"I can't, even if I want to. I have another life, another family. I can't just show up with two more children out of nowhere." He looked at Grandma for the first time.

"Out of nowhere?" Grandma snapped, throwing her scarf on the ground. "*Out of nowhere?*" She shoved off the chair as though she would charge him right there and then. Her eyes widened with outrage; a fury so powerful that her gaze should have made him burst into flames. I'd never seen Grandma so mad. "They are not just two more children out of nowhere; these are your children, Daniel, your firstborns," Grandma hissed between grinding teeth, muffling her anger to avoid the attention of others present at the funeral.

Our father? I blinked up at him in confusion.

"I am sorry," he muttered, his tone complementing his expressionless face. Nothing left to say, he walked away.

Grandma's hands shook as her petite frame trembled. "Bastard," she mumbled. Her eyes brimming, she gracefully slipped her handkerchief from her purse and blotted the oncoming tears with a slow dab.

Brian was quiet, more confused than me about all that had happened. The emotional stress from the loss of Momma weighed heavier on him. Shell shocked, he sat slumped in the chair with his head hung low. Shivering, he managed to hold off from making a sound for the better part of a minute. Then he released the most pitiful wail I'd ever heard. Everyone stopped what they were doing and turned toward us.

It frightened me. With dewy eyes, I grabbed Brian and gripped him to my chest, one hand petting his brow as I murmured whatever comfort a nine-year-old could offer. Grandma Ivie rushed over, put her arms around us both, and whispered hoarsely through a tight throat, "Everything will be okay. You will be okay. I'll make sure of it."

Soon Brian quieted. As the stragglers stopped to share their condolences, he kept close to me, focused on the ground.

A man wearing a pair of jeans and a dark suit jacket sat on the empty chair beside us. "I'm Dal, an old friend of your moms from a while back."

I had never seen his face before Momma's funeral. Mixed in with the people I knew, two more of these old friends had come up. I remembered each name as it was told to me: Dal, Ottis, Axel. Old friends, they'd said. I must have nodded but didn't understand.

When Daimhin approached us, Brian and I both jumped up to sandwich him in our hugs. We knew Daimhin; he always had time for us and treated us well. He was a strong man, but his trembling lips that day told me he desperately wanted to cry.

He held us tightly. "Stay strong, kids. And remember, I'm here for you. If either of you ever need anything, call me?" His eyes pleaded as he reached into his pocket for a pen and paper. He jotted his number down on the back of a random business card and gave it to me.

Gazing up at him, I asked, "Anytime?"

"Anytime."

After the funeral, people stopped by the house to pay a visit. They brought cooked meals and envelopes, asked if there was anything needed, anything to help Grandma Ivie. Brian sat on the couch quietly, caught up in a sad world of his own as I longed for our old life and everything about it.

Memories pricked my mind. I disappeared into the basement, home to the packed remnants from our old house. I rummaged through the still-sealed boxes. One labeled Nancy's stuff caught my eye. Ripping off the tape, I yearned to embrace whatever was in the box, things most precious to Momma. Right on top, I found a book with *The Holy Bible* printed in the middle of cover. At the bottom, engraved in silver letters, was the name *Nancy Bremen*.

"But Momma's last name was Hellington." Perhaps it belonged to some unknown namesake of Momma's.

I unfastened the Velcro strip which held the broken lock, opened the book, and flipped through the handwritten pages. I'd never read a Bible, though Grandma Ivie often mentioned events from the Good Book. Even when Brian and I attended church with her, I would sleep for long spells, then wake up whenever Grandma nudged me to sit up straight and pay attention. She was a practicing Christian and did her best to lead us into faith. She often referred to verses from the Bible and would at times narrate the stories from it. At that time, to me, the Bible was a collection of stories with morals, a book with lots of *don'ts* that I didn't like.

Contrary to Grandma, Momma wasn't much into religion, but still she had a Bible. Perhaps a gift from Grandma Ivie or, like the cover said, it belonged to some Nancy Bremen rather than Momma.

I placed the book back in the box and started ravaging through her other things: an old pen, a broken hair clip, a ring. That beautiful ring had a bright red stone, a fine and expensive piece of jewelry, but I didn't remember Momma ever wearing it.

Voices came from the kitchen upstairs. I held the ring tight in my hand and listened. Grandma Ivie asked Brian where I was, and I heard him reply that he hadn't seen me.

"Brea come on; time for supper," Grandma Ivie yelled in her smooth tone.

Supper? I didn't realize I'd been in the basement for quite that long. Once the Bible was safely in Momma's box, I uncrossed my legs and leaped up in a hurried scramble. Taking the steps two at a time, I headed up stairs.

When I opened the door into the kitchen, Grandma Ivie stood there with her hands on her wide hips. "What are you doing down in the basement, Brea?"

"Nothing, looking through Momma's things. What are we going to do with it all?"

"Nothing yet, haven't taken the time to get around to it. You be careful down there; there's stuff all over the place."

"Okay, Grandma, I will." I wanted to ask her about the woman's name on the Bible, which had been tearing at me since I found the book. Uneasy about the question, I decided to go the route of not caring so much. "Who is Nancy Bremen, Grandma?"

"Why, that's your mother," she replied.

"Bremen?"

"Her father, your grandfather, and me, that's our last name. When your mother married your father, her last name changed to his, Hellington, like yours."

A nervous laugh wheezed from me. "How come I never knew your last name was Bremen? I always thought it was the same as ours."

"I don't know, baby; I guess you never noticed."

"So, does this mean you had another name before you got married?"

"Smart girl!" Her praise felt like warm honey on my wounded soul. "Yes, I had a different last name before I married."

"What happened to our grandfather? Where is he now? You never talk about him."

"Brea, your grandfather passed away a long time ago. He was a young man, only forty-one years old. Your momma was about your age then, maybe a few years older," said Grandma Ivie in a shallow voice as her eyes shined with tears. "We can talk another time. Come on; let's eat." She grabbed my hand and led me to the dinner table where Brian sat waiting.

"I'm starving," he grumbled.

"I know, Brian, but we were waiting on your sister."

Brian smirked at me, and I frowned back playfully. I had so many more questions, but seeing how it made Grandma Ivie sad, I decided not to ask her.

***

Thirteen years old, I'm a teenager! We're teenagers!

This birthday had me more excited than I had been in a long while. Grandma Ivie, Brian, and I arranged a small birthday celebration. It wasn't much, a few classmates and friends from the neighborhood, but I wished Momma was alive to celebrate with us.

Early that morning, I woke up eager, ready to decorate for our guests. Grandma Ivie was already working in the kitchen by the time I hustled downstairs. She smiled up at me and pulled me into a warm embrace.

"Happy birthday! A teenager, huh?" she said against my head.

I smiled sheepishly. Over the next few hours, we put the finishing touches on the food and the room, then waited for our guests to arrive. The first few guests didn't impress me, girls from school who were not my friends.

Even so, they jumped at the invite once I told them Brian and I were having a birthday party.

More people showed than I expected. Right when the party was getting into full swing, I heard a voice I recognized all too well! When Daimhin's low baritone boomed across a room, Brian and I always ran out from whatever rocks we were under. He walked into the living room. I stood in the doorway, receiving the guests, trying to be as nice as possible, just like a grown-up. As Grandma Ivie had said, "You are thirteen now, not a kid anymore."

But on seeing Daimhin, Brian and I scrambled toward him without a care who was watching, just like old times when he came visiting Momma with treats all those years ago. While wooing Momma, Daimhin had taken us for ice cream in the park and read to us at times before bed. He was always kind to us when Momma was alive, more so now that she was gone.

Daimhin pulled us into a group hug. I snuggled close to him, taking in a whiff of his cologne. I had always liked the way he smelled, soft musk and wood; it was comforting.

"How are my not-so-little ones doing?" he asked when we finally peeled ourselves off him.

"Ew, Daimhin. We're not kids." Brian teased.

"Anyway, I got you 'not-kids' a little something." Daimhin said as he pointed toward two gifts in the doorway. They were big, body size, and covered with sheets. He walked up and stood right between them. With a smile on his face, one hand on each of the gifts, he paused for a moment as we watched in excitement. Then, like a magician performing a trick, he pulled away the sheets. They moved up with a rough swish. Before our eyes sat two electric scooters, a black one and a red one, the latest model, something we never would have bought for ourselves.

Brian and I squealed loudly, eager to go for a ride.

"Black is mine," I shouted.

"Nooooooo," Brian complained. "You get the red one. Black is my favorite color."

Sensing the impending hostilities, Daimhin walked up to me, smiling. He bent and whispered in my ear, "Red is my personal favorite. I got that one for you."

"Ok, I get the red one," I said softly while he playfully winked at me. "Thanks, Daimhin." I hugged him again.

"Yeah, thanks, Daimhin. I'm going outside to go ride this." Brian walked away from the two of us.

"Where's your grandma, dear?" Daimhin asked, turning toward me.

"I guess she's in the kitchen."

"All right. I need to go say hi." He gave me another hug before he went to find her.

I smiled as I watched him walk toward the kitchen, then I joined the other guests at the party. Walking through the hallway, it felt great seeing all these people here. The last time we had so many visitors was the funeral.

While our guests talked, laughed, and enjoyed sodas and birthday cake, I heard girls giggling, hyperexcited, in the other room. They stared at Brian as he fooled around with his scooter. The way they ogled him all dreamy-eyed, I realized why all these girls had come to this party despite not being actual friends of mine. They rolled the tips of their hair around their fingers and flashed bashful half-smiles when he glanced their way.

I had to admit, my brother was a cute boy, with his curly black hair and olive complexion. He had sparkling white teeth that gleamed when he smiled, even though he didn't do enough to keep them that way.

The girls kept drooling over him, but Brian was busy riding his scooter, one with the wind. I watched him, glad to see him out of his room, happy for once. And for a split second, I saw what they all saw: happy, carefree Brian, young and bold and growing strong.

Once our classmates left, Daimhin called for us to say his goodbyes.

I clasped my arms around his waist; I always hated when he had to go. "Will you be back to visit soon?"

Daimhin chuckled, soft and kind, amused by my enthusiasm. "Maybe in another month. There is a lot going on at work, but if you need me, I'm just a phone call away." He kissed me on top of the head. On his way out, he gave Brian's shoulder a gentle squeeze and told him to be careful with the new ride. "And make sure you always wear your helmet."

With that our last guest left the house. Moments later, Grandma popped in with a garbage bag, ready to clean up.

I got up and stacked a few cups and plates together.

Grandma Ivie shooed me away. "It's your birthday. Go have fun. I'll clean up."

"You sure?" I asked, dropping some disposable cups into the bag.

"Yes, sweetie. Now get going." She swatted me with the napkin in her hands as though I were a fly pestering her.

I slinked off to my room, took out a book from my bookshelf, and opened it to where I'd left off. Investigative fiction was an addiction, my second favorite pastime after watching crime procedurals on TV.